FAMILY BUSINESS

BY

TOM BOURGUILLON

Dedication

In memory of my father, Jean Thomas Bourguillon.
To my mother Carole, thank you for your love and support.
To my sister Peggy for being the best sister in the world – there,
it's official.
I love you all, always.

Also, I would like to give thanks to God,
through whom all things are possible.

Acknowledgements

To Brian Dennis and Cornelius Medas for your support, providing me with feedback for my ideas, giving me great one liners, and giving helpful insights on the on-goings of New York life.

To Tom Gaydos and Neil Agni for their support and great one liners.

To the members of NaNo and the Fairfield County Writer's Group for their insight, advice, encouragement, and sense of humor, and especially to Catherine Kane and Charles Muir for your guidance and leadership.

To Phalla Touch for thinking of me when forwarding the Udemy.com coupon from LivingSocial.com; it motivated me when I needed it.

To Steve Acorn from the Novel Writing Workshop on Udemy.com, I would like to thank him for a wonderful on-line class and for answering my questions.

To Juliette Eisner from VICE for allowing me to reference their "Fist Fighting on Christmas: A Peruvian Tradition" YouTube video: http://www.youtube.com/watch?v=mKjSyZhIIiw. They provided me ideas for a more entertaining character.

My thanks to Katherine Campbell for editing my story; your insight really helped bring out more of my story's potential.

Table of Contents

Chapter 1: The People's Army

SURVIVAL—not money or fame—it's survival that makes a warlord. I once thought blood diamonds were the life blood of General Abasi's army, but then I was taught the General's version of Ubuntu—the people's alliance under his order, so that all lives can improve.

I see his version of it now, as I sit on the tail end of a jeep as Abasi drives. I watch him smoke his cigar without a care in the world. The only thing worthy of his company is his favorite AK-47 assault rifle resting on the passenger seat.

I have only his young, human shield to give me company. By which I mean he has been looking at me since we left the camp, but I keep myself busy looking around the area, planning for a retreat if it's necessary; should the mission go badly, I like having my options.

"Why do you always look around?" The teen's frankness gets my attention.

I smile at the young teen. "I love South Africa."

Abasi laughs. Slow at first, then loudly when his human shield has no response for my quick wit. Anything that makes Abasi laughs is a good thing. Otherwise, Abasi's mood is dead serious when he is working to be South Africa's next political leader the traditional way for a warlord; maim and kill, starting with the smallest and weakest groups around his territory. But despite his plans, one day someone else will take his place. Every king dies.

I look at the young teen's new AKM-63 in his small hands. I imagine he's already prayed to survive his recent promotion. I look up to the night sky and all the stars lighting it up like twinkling crystals; it's beautiful but I'm still anxious to leave for America. My attention goes towards a large, bright, orange fireball from an explosion ahead us.

"The scouting party is starting the attack without us, General?"

Abasi laughs before taking a long puff of his cigar. I turn to the human shield. His wide-eyed expression on his face while watching the explosion shows me the rare glimpse of his innocence as the horrific screams and gunfire in the on-coming village draw near.

Nothing new to me, though. Abasi's small scouting group slips across the rebels' defenses and blows up any defensive vehicles. Then they'll move in during the chaos, jam radio communications, and use fear and intimidation to their advantage when taking down targets; it is guerilla tactics 101. But thanks to my training they're stealthier than any African government soldier or rebel.

This will be the fifth village of rebels in Southern Zimbabwe out of the fifteen raids Abasi plans to make in the area, but I mentally prepare myself as if it's the first. It's becoming harder to not factor in the human lives but labeling them as targets is helping me, like I was in some zombie or horror movie. I have to do whatever it takes to get the job done, as the business of war is good for my boss's business.

Abasi stops the jeep, throws his cigar out the window, takes his rifle, and gets out. We know our roles; I'm to snipe from above and the human shield follows the general. I exchange a look with the teen and try to encourage him with a pat on the back before he jumps out of the jeep, but he only looks at me strangely as I give him the thumbs up.

"Go get them." It isn't a football speech, but I'm extending an olive branch.

Abasi laughs at my attempt and walks away. The boy jumps off the jeep and follows him, as does the remainder of his squad from the jeeps that stop and park behind us. I go into my sniper case at my feet, open it, and take out Black Widow, my black VSSK Vychlop sniper rifle. I look over her beautiful details before I pocket a small box of ammo, close the sniper case, jump off the jeep, and run to the nearby hill as per the mission briefing.

After a quick sprint to the top, I kneel down and roll several large stones away. As I lie down and plant Black Widow softly on the ground, I start to calm my breathing. I see through the night vision scope that the village's guard has no chance against Abasi's men. They are outnumbered and out gunned, thanks to my employer. Abasi doesn't need me for this, but he keeps me around for everything he does, like a belt around a hip when the pants already possess suspenders. It's my reward for saving his life from a soldier his previous human shield got in front of but didn't have time to even raise his gun up against.

I completely calm my breathing. Then I aim at my first target and fire. He falls like a bag of rocks onto the car he was hiding beside. I adjust my hold for the recoil and pick targets off one by one. It's almost too easy. A few of them get enough sense to make a run for it, but Abasi's men catch them in the crossfire and riddle their bodies with bullets. Their bodies fall to the ground like a ballet of death. I make a mental note to teach Abasi's men better bullet management.

"Come on…give up."

I look for another target and I see a flash at the top, open window of a two-story home. I make out a rebel hiding inside a house as he kills two of Abasi's men. I end his life, watch his body fall out the window, and fall onto the ground headfirst.

"Oh yeah, he's dead."

I watch the remaining rebels flee into a jeep on the other side of the village, too quickly for me to take a clear shot as the dust flies in all directions from the tires. Another uprising to swat later, I imagine. I scan the village as Abasi's men walk the streets without hindrance, pulling the hurt rebels into a line up and forcing them to kneel on the ground. The butterflies in my stomach tell me that the night isn't over yet.

As I relax my finger on the trigger, I watch as Abasi walks out from his hiding place along with his human shield. He waves me down. Before I do anything else, I scan the village and the other houses. No signs of life.

I get up, put Black Widow on my shoulder, and walk down the hill. Walking into the village and stepping over the scorched pieces of brick on the ground, I can see the inside of the guard's office the scouts blew up before we arrived; the communication system and jail cell inside are still burning and smoking into the night sky. Then I watch as Abasi's men finish rounding up the rebels into a line, about to declare Abasi's rule.

The rebels are skinny, feeble, and their ribs are showing through shirts that have rips and tears. They look nothing like Abasi's well-fed thoroughbred soldiers; healthy, strong, and carrying weapons like action heroes from the movie imports I brought them.

I look at Abasi standing comfortably, from what I can tell, close to a burning car. The fire light is highlighting the salt and pepper colors of his hair and beard. For a man that has just won an easy victory, the frown on his face makes me nervous. He shoves his human shield ahead of him with more force than required for a teen his size; the boy nearly topples over.

I look at the human shield and see him for the thirteen-year-old boy that he truly is as he trembles while holding up his rifle at the rebels looking back at him, begging for their lives. Abasi yell at him in their language and then I finally understand the situation; it took me two months to learn Afrikaans but it was a worthy investment. The boy never took a shot with the rifle and Abasi needs to know if it works. But more importantly, he needs to know if the boy has any guts to use it.

My heart aches for the boy, he has never been taught to control his nerves; until now. And as he continues to shake, I imagine that will pose as a problem if he still wants to be in a militant army, especially Abasi's army.

"General, if you want me to…"

Abasi raises his hand at me briefly and then lowers it. That is the end of the conversation. No one argues with Abasi and lives to see their families. He continues to yell at the boy with so much anger that spit flies from his mouth. But that is textbook Abasi. He paid for the guns, provided for his soldiers' training, and gave them food and shelter. Not to do what you're told will make you an outcast by right. Abasi slaps the boy's head and immediately makes him tear up.

I look away as the boy wipes his tears away; it brings up too much of the wrong memories. Abasi's men aren't that decent and they snicker at the boy. They have forgotten how to be soft. Their black shirts, black pants, and boots are from the fallen soldiers before them; part of Abasi's training to not fear death is both cruel and genius.

I look at the rebels, at the panic and defeat in their eyes. I assume they understood their situation when they weren't hog tied; no one worth the rope is meant to get a bullet, Abasi 101. At least through me they wouldn't be whimpering right now, waiting to die by a child's hand. I look back at Abasi as he looks at the boy with an ice cold stare. Then Abasi looks at me, then I understood the situation the boy is in; if he didn't pull the trigger at the rebels, I would pull my trigger at him. That shit isn't going to happen.

"Soldiers keep the peace! Soldiers enforce the will of the people!" The boy looks at me as I raise Black Widow in the air. "And the people are General Abasi!" Abasi's men yell Abasi's name in response, raising their rifles in the air. "Ubuntu!" Abasi's men chant the same, louder when Abasi raises his rifle in the air and chants along.

The boy takes long, deep breathes as he aims the rifle at the rebels. He opens fire. The rebels scream as they are killed in a stream of bullets. We all chant and applaud the boy. He smiles and looks at me with a large grin as tears stream down his round face. Abasi's men start laughing as Abasi rubs the boy's head like the proud owner of a dog that just learned a new trick.

With a smile on his face, Abasi tells his men in Afrikaans to sweep the area for more rebels. I don't say anything; better for them to keep busy and pretend to have some value than be left bored and anxious to kill something. Abasi walks to me, slaps my back hard, and laughs as he walks towards a flaming building. I watch him light another cigar that he pulls from his shirt pocket and start to walk around. I follow him.

The boy walks to my side. "My name is Lungile."

I turn to him. "The Vulture." I make a bird sound and make him smile. "But seriously, my name is DeAndre." We shake hands, then he runs and catches up to Abasi's side and his destiny.

Chapter 2: Reporting Back

MY PLANE lands on time and I'm glad to be back in the United States. Even though the general's new orders for weapons will make my stay short, right now all is right in the world. After the delay at the airport terminal because of the updated x-ray security scanners people were trying to avoid, I'm happy to be in Melrose in the Bronx.

And even in the hot morning, summer sun, I see young women singing along to loud, American pop music as they lower their windows in their cars; I miss the various New York accents. After my stomach is full of hot chocolate and doughnuts and I'm caught up on the Mets, I have no more excuses not to see Frankie the Bull, a capodecina of the Abdone family.

Fifteen minutes later, I park a few spots away from the Lucky Guy club. Three wise guys are casually sitting on one of the outside tables, smoking and probably chatting away about whatever checkered plans they have done, are planning to do, or will do. I get out of my car and walk toward the front door. I don't give them a reason to look twice at me as I unbutton my suit jacket wide open before I walk inside.

Despite it being a club for connected guys with a blend of colognes that burns my nostrils, looking at the forty year old women in tight jeans passing me by makes me forget about the pain. I watch as the aging beauties work the room for their fifteen minutes of fame, free drinks, or whatever passes the time.

I walk into the hallway to the left and towards the back room. As soon as I take a step inside the back room a large, white hand is slapped on my chest. I immediately raise my hands as Frankie's top muscle pats me down.

"How are you doing, Tony?"

Tony has kept up with his girth and his purple running suit can't hide it as a little fat dangles over his pants. There's been no changes made to backroom in the six months I've been gone; now that I think about it nothing has changed since I started working for Frankie five years ago. It still has the same background designs and pictures of Italian actors and figures. I imagine the same rules apply. To be in this room you either have business to attend to or you're a big spender that's going to spend money on card games, escorts, a better lever of food and drinks, or all of the above.

Tony finishes patting me down. I only had to identify my cell phone. Tony moves aside, sits down on a nearby chair, and reads the *New York Post* after taking a quick peek at the security monitor near him. I can see Frankie's balding, marble head at the end of room from here; his slick black hair isn't what it used to be. His thick, dark eyebrows make Frankie hard to miss. He's playing cards with his crew; I imagine they're letting him win. He has the young women of the week by his side, as always. He turns his head, spots me, and he grins.

Frankie mockingly salutes me as he yells, "Yo! Look whose back...Mandela!" He looks back at his crew and they laugh along with him.

His crew always laughs at his jokes, like it's a job requirement. Frankie's guys are hoodlums just like him. That's why I see them get along more often than not. But they do respect him and get paid well for it; considering the thousand dollar suits they are wearing. His crew consists of well known wheelmen, strongmen, gunmen, and killers in the criminal world, but they all should know if anyone gets on his bad side they become a headline in the paper the next day. That's what I was told on my first day.

Prior to that I thought guys like Frankie didn't go far in the mafia, from what I've seen in the movies anyways. But working with him over the years, I've seen him make things happen and earn a lot of money in the process. I give credit where credit is due; Frankie works hard for what he has and fights hard to keep it.

I walk towards Frankie, briefly looking around at the other tables full of fancy drinks, food, and men in suits with silly grins on their faces as they watch beautiful women dancing in front of them. I see Tanya, the Russian charmer, working a client with more white hair than black on his head. She's laughing at whatever bad joke he's telling her while he's looking down the slit of her black dress and enjoying that her high heels are rubbing against his leg. I assume because of her work ethic that the long, white fur coat that is on the coat rack is hers. I look away, remembering how I often scare off her clients.

Tanya laughs again. I take a quick look back at her; I can't help it. She's downplaying her beautiful bust, but it's hard not to look at her sexy vanilla legs showing through the slit of her dress. As she continues to win the client over with a bright smile, but she holds his wrinkled hands while he talks to her, keeping them in place on her knee, and that's it; that's what I keep telling myself.

With all the escorts with short, blonde bangs around the room, Tanya always stands out with her long, black, wavy hair. In any room Tanya stands out, thanks to the teachings of her idol Marilyn Monroe. Tanya is tall and elegant like a stunning model, wearing red lipstick and blush. And yet amongst the sea of escorts in the room with body treatments, she can get my attention with a sweet smile. And unlike the other escorts from Europe, Tanya is teaching herself English. Brains and beauty always does it for me, that's why I remember the little details she shares so that I can leave a good impression on her.

I walk to Frankie's table. Red, white, and blue chips are spread across the table, but are mostly in a mix pile in front of Frankie. I look over the table at Frankie's hand. They're playing poker and Frankie should be losing his shirt with only a pair of eights and no chance of a better hand, knowing his luck. I once saw him buy a new car and get into an accident the same day, a simple fender bender. And after the repair, his car gets side swiped by an unknown driver in the middle of the night; I wouldn't leave my information either.

"Hello, Mr. Mancini." I state with respect.

Frankie keeps his eyes on his cards. "Are our friends in the south happy with the first set of product?"

"Very happy, they'll…"

"Yeah, yeah…five cards."

He is being risky, but I see Frankie's hand go from bad to worse. He has no hand; his only chance of winning high card is to follow it with a threat. Before I see how it turns out, I hear a ruckus behind me. I turn around and I see Tanya getting slapped to the floor. I take a step forward without thinking.

"Hey yo! Where you going, Mandela?" Frankie asks with ferocity in his voice.

I stop in place. "Sorry, sir," I reply.

"You ain't in Africa anymore! Actions have real consequences here!"

I stand still as the man yells at Tanya, calling her a tease and a Russian whore; it's hard for me to just be standing there. Frankie snaps his fingers and I watch Tony jump up from his seat, walk over to the client, push him to the bar, and punch him in the stomach twice. That's all that is needed to make the client docile.

"A little bruise, but it'll heal. If the guy comes back causing trouble, we'll take care of it, understand? I don't want to hear of trouble from you," Frankie tells me.

"Of course, I'm Mandela."

Frankie slaps his cards down on the table hard and I hear the chips scatter across the table and it gains my attention, and everyone else's, then he points at me. "Don't get smart with me!"

I see that he's still as intense as the bull on his gold pinky ring. And, like a bull, there's no point fighting one when it's engaged and its eyes are glaring at you.

"I'm sorry…"

"I don't want to hear it! Get the hell out of my sight! We'll talk later about business, when I don't feel like smashing your teeth in!" He waves me off with disregard like I'm some bum off the street.

I turn and walk to Tanya as she stands up. Tony tugs the client by the shoulder and walks him out. There's fear on the man's face and pee cascading down his pants. I make mental notes to call him Pee Pants around the club later, enough times that people make sure it sticks to him for the rest of his life or until he makes it up to Tanya.

As everyone goes back to their business, I grab the cold, wet towel that the bartender already prepared and offer it to Tanya. She stares at me with her brown eyes while her chin swells red, but she does swipe the towel from my hand and places it on her chin.

I go a little numb inside, but I keep a brave face on. "Are you..."

She turns around, walks to the coat rack, snatches the fur coat off the hanger, and walks out of the room. I hear laughter from Frankie's crew behind me; the loudest of all is Frankie. I walk after Tanya, ready to face the music.

I pass by Tony on his way back inside. "Thanks for the rescue, Tony."

He gives me a wink before I walk outside and stand behind Tanya as she hails for a taxi. "Tanya! My car is right there." I point to my silver Audi S6 even though she's not looking at me. "Don't be stupid!"

"Don't call me stupid," she barks as she finally looks at me.

"I'm not...I'm just saying..."

"It's very difficult for me in America, you know," she yells before she turns back around and continues to hail for a taxi, failing to realize, in her anger, that a woman with her look and with a bruise on her face is usually ignored; New York taxis usually ignore fares with that kind of drama. "Because I can't find words at once…and take many time to talk, don't call me stupid! Ok?"

"I didn't."

As I hear her mumble something angrily in Russian, I know this won't be the last I hear of this. But to make her happy I whistle for a taxi and flash a few bills that I take out from my inside jacket and a taxi stops in front of her.

As she opens the door, I say, "I was thinking I'd pay for your time for three days." She stands still. "You can sleep in for all three days if you're still angry at me…wearing comfortable pajamas all day…"

I watch her turn around with her hand out. "Money."

"Ok, Tanya. Have it your way." I fight a smile as I take out more money from my money clip, separating the fifties as I walk closer to her.

"Want sex with me?" She asks.

I sigh and start separating the hundreds, but stop as she grabs several bills in a large lump from my clip, more than enough to cover the taxi fare to Connecticut and back. She turns around and gets in the taxi, slamming the door. I put the money clip back in my pocket and bend down with a pleasant smile, even though she's looking forward as she's giving the taxi driver instructions.

"I'll see you at my Brownstone apartment, then? You still have the key, right?" She doesn't reply, so I knock on the window. I see her sigh but she doesn't reply or even turn to look at me, so keep knocking against the window with purpose. "Hello! Honey, sweetheart…"

She slowly looks at me with narrowed eyes as I stop knocking and pucker my lips. I watch as her window lowers and I smile widely. "You came back unhurt, don't push luck."

As the taxi drives away, I stand up straight and I gauge my age as the soreness from my latest adventures is still present in my back; I hate being in my thirties. "I know you want me!" Tanya sticks her hand out the window and flips me the bird, keeping it visible until the taxi turns the corner. "She wants me."

After a brief stretch, getting confirmation that I'm only getting older by the second as the pain doesn't go away, I start to wonder what my friend Miguel is doing right now. I make a mental note to see him later, but right now I decide to go back inside the club and start rumors about Pee Pants at the bar.

Chapter 3: Sisterly Love

I WAKE UP in my bed with Tanya's good morning kiss on my cheek. Her arm resting on my side, her lightly brushing hand against the hairs of my chest makes me tingle in all the right places. I look at her and she looks back at me with a courteous smile. It eases the memory of the previous day, considering her chin has a thin white layer of her citrus crème remedy.

"Miss me?" I ask, giving her a wink.

"I don't forgot to enjoy myself in bathroom yesterday," Tanya replies.

"Do you forgive me?" I would do almost anything to keep her looking at me with those sexy mocha eyes of hers.

"Maybe yes, maybe no," she replies.

I hold her hand and kiss it. "Please."

"Maybe yes, maybe no," she replies with a slight grin.

"That's fair enough." I move her hand aside and sit up. I move the covers aside as I turn to the end of the bed and stretch my legs for a moment. Her gentle hand on my bare back keeps me still. As does her soft fingers tracing the wings of my back tattoo; my tattoo artist, Randel, made a special trip to Africa for a fair price.

"More feathers, please tell me this meaning?" Tanya asks.

"More tragedies than I thought." The bed shakes slightly and I welcome her warm arms as they slowly wrap around my neck. She softly kisses my neck. "You forgive me then?"

"It's too hot to be in doghouse longtime," she whispers tenderly, following that she tells me in Russian that she misses kissing my brown skin. She then whispers a plea, "Ten minutes."

As she rubs my chest with her hands and kisses my neck, I reply back, "Two minutes." I let her pull me back into bed.

She sits on top of me and smiles, the creases at the corners of her mouth add to her sex appeal. She orders, "Five minutes," as she takes off her silk pajama top.

I'm in awe of her raw beauty. "Two minutes and thirty seconds."

AT THE FRONT door of the Lucky Guy, I look through the window when I find out the doors are locked. My curiosity was already piqued when my usual spot is taken and I have to pay a few extra bucks to some kids to keep their butts on a nearby stoop while looking after my car a few blocks away. I'm tempted to sneak around the back and peek through the windows, but the cameras will get me into trouble. Besides, I don't know what to do with the tray of coffees and the box of doughnuts I was told to buy.

There isn't any activity inside. It's seven in the morning, but there should be at least someone standing behind the bar for the early bird drunks. Tony suddenly walks in front of the door, signaling me to step away; he finally caught me in the monitor. When I step away, he opens the door and steps outside.

As he looks around, confirming there aren't people lurking to make a hit, I see that he's dressed up in a black suit and leather shoes. I've only seen Tony dress up on special occasions or when he's sent out to scare people into submission. We're almost matching, except I'm wearing a blue shirt and he's wearing a white shirt, and I'm not the one hundred pounds overweight. I want to make a joke about being twins, but the frustration on his face tells me not to bother.

"I got business with Frankie…and I got the coffee and doughnuts…" Tony takes the coffee and doughnuts, but as soon as he steps inside the door is immediately shut and locked. "I'll just wait here then, ok?" I joke to deaf ears.

Suddenly having nine thousand six hundred dollars in my pocket to have Tanya to myself for a few extra days sounds like a bad idea. But I'm an outcast in their world and I have to wait outside like a sucker. All I want to do is be back in Tanya's company on the couch and forget about the world, but first things first, I have to hand deliver the money.

One of many things the movies got right, people like Frankie don't care about your problems; they just want their money. I would walk back to my car to check on it, but most people know not to mess with the cars from the Lucky Guy, even with associates like me; word would get to Grand Street in Little Italy and then people would start disappearing.

As I pace back and forth on the sidewalk, checking for any smudges on my shoes, my phone vibrates in my pocket. I take it out and read the text message from Tanya's dog sitter, confirming that Tanya has picked up Urola and that my card is being charged for additional surcharges for a list of cleaning and shoe damage.

I sigh and put my phone back in my pocket. I like Urola; I love dogs in general. But this little black Russian Tsvetnaya Bolonka is truly a little bear. She's friendly, loyal, and good with children, but everything else is subject to being treated like a chew toy if left alone and without protection.

A black limo drives in front as a few old white men in suits walk out of the club. I've never seen them before; they're too calm, classy, and skinny to be in Frankie's crew. They keep their eyes on me, which makes me look away. I don't look back at them until they climb inside the limo and drive away, giving them a respectful distance.

I watch as this process continues several times, with a different combination of people and newly waxed vehicles. Some men leave with younger women, some leave alone, some with a crew of five men around them loosening their ties as soon as they walk out the door. This has too big, syndicate big.

Tony knocks on the front door's window to get my attention and waves me in. I walk inside and Tony is talking to some elderly guys in wrinkled suits, but I keep standing near the door waiting for him to search me.

But instead, he waves me away like some big shot. Then he continues talking and the wise guys laugh at whatever joke he's made. They pat his shoulder favorably. I've watched Tony over the years; he's earned the complete confidence and respect of everyone that comes in and out of the club with his words or his fists.

And while Tony has always been social, he's ready at a moment's notice to help out anyone he knows that's in trouble. And to my liking is that he never makes fun of anyone else. But he usually avoids crowds because he's an easy target for jokes, so I wonder why he's talking so openly right now.

I walk towards the back as I hear the wise guys laugh at Tony's next joke behind me. Before I walk inside the backroom I can hear that Frankie is yelling at someone, half in English and half in Italian. From what I can understand the meeting didn't go well and he was called a disgrace. I can't make out the details of his offense, but I then hear something about another captain in another family and his daughter from college; that's all I need to hear. I walk inside and Frankie is pacing back and forth.

"Can you believe that shit? Manhattan is out of my reach now? I give and I give and I give to those greedy pigs every month! And now I can only do business in the Bronx?" Frankie picks up a chair and throws it at the bar. The chair breaks several bottles before it falls to the floor. He ignores his crew's pleas to calm down and throws another chair, breaking a row of bottles this time.

He turns around in my direction and looks at me with wild eyes; it unsettles me. "Yo! Come here!" He snaps his fingers and points to his feet.

I quickly walk to him, but I keep my calm while unbuttoning the buttons on my jacket. "Yes, Mr...."

"Never mind that...has anyone approached you on the African deal?"

"No, should I worry..."

"Worry if you're lying to me." He points to my face and looks me dead in the eye.

"No one," I answer.

Taking a step closer he tells me, "From now on only my guys are going to handle any deals in Africa. Anything you got…names, e-mails, whatever…you give to me."

"No disrespect, but General Abasi doesn't like…"

He slaps the left side of head hard; I keep my calm by looking away—I have to. "I don't give a damn who he wants to work with! If he wants my guns, he's going to do things my way! Understand? Hey, understand?"

I look up at him as he looks at me intensely. "Yes sir," I answer like a humbled officer in the Army.

He steps away, turns to his table, picks up his drink, and gulps half of it. "And get Tanya over here in an hour. The girls are going to work over time from now on."

"That's why I'm here. I'm paying for Tanya for a few days…"

"Then pay me twenty thousand."

The number nearly shatters the budget I set aside for myself this month. "Twenty thousand? Hey, Frankie, come on…"

"What did you call me, you shit?"

"No…you're right…

"You forget who you're talking to," he says, glaring at me.

"I'm just saying, I've been a good earner and I have expenses…"

"One call and…ah, Pee Pants…is that what you've been calling him?" I swallow hard as he looks at me with a sly grin; I did too good of a job. "Yeah…he can come up with that money and a prepaid room. My protection is stopping that from happening."

"You can take it out of my cut from the African..."

"I already did...salute." He finishes the drink and puts the glass on the table. "Now get the hell out of here."

I turn around and walk toward the door. I hear Frankie say, in Italian to his crew, that I have no balls and they laugh; he's called me worse. I walk out of the backroom. The conversation is more draining than I realize. As I walk pass Tony, we exchange looks of understanding; the ship is starting to sink.

I FINALLY drive up to my Brownstone apartment in Yorkville in the Upper East Side, only to be forced to drive in a loop to look for parking, for twenty minutes—unbelievable. I decide to just go to the parking lot until I see the bright yellow lights from a towing truck pulling a car that parked too close to the hydrant across from my apartment. I smile guilt free as it gets towed; the several one hundred and sixty dollar pink tickets on its dashboard, with "Violation" in big text, were enough warning.

I quickly get the spot before the driver behind me steals it. The other driver, an old woman in glasses, looks at me with disappointment as she passes me by. I look away and don't exchange glances, but I still put my car in park and turn off the engine. I get out of my car and lock it, carrying only the small paper package of Russian movie imports, fresh from the Fordham Plaza for Tanya.

Other than any movie starring Marilyn Monroe, science fiction movies from the seventies and eighties with Andrei

Tarkovsky as director will serve as a better apology than anything I can say and will earn me brownie points. That is my hope at least. I'm glad the cool air is blowing against my moist back before I open the door. I'm assuming that Tanya hasn't put the central air on high yet.

"Nia, did you tell me you were coming here tonight?" Seeing Nia in my apartment is one thing, but her having tea with Tanya at the dining room table is the last thing I expected. Tanya could have at least been using the generic guest tea cups and not my purple Legle Parma tea cups and saucers.

"And this is what I've been talking about, Tanya," Nia comments as she points at me briefly.

I sigh as I look behind Nia and see two bright pink-colored suitcases on the floor. There has to be a story behind her presence, I just wonder if it requires a court appearance by me. "Had another party in your apartment in Washington Heights? Is the building still standing?"

I watch as Tanya stand up without the usually welcoming smile on her face, walk to me, and give me a hug; her arms affectionately around my neck as her chest lightly presses against mine. "I'm sorry DeAndre," Tanya says with a little grief.

I hug her back, putting my hands around her waist, but whisper with concern, "What's the matter?"

"Our parents are dead," Nia comments before she sniffles.

"Nia, come on now…if this is a joke…"

"You didn't check your machine for messages have you?"

"No, I…no…" I see Nia's eyes water and I know she's not telling a bad joke or scam so that she can crash at my place. I can't think of anything to say despite my lips moving.

As I try to get my brain to start to functioning again, Tanya closes and locks the door behind me. As Tanya takes the paper package of movies from my hand, she whispers, "I give you tea." Her voice is just as soothing as the kiss on my cheek that she gives me before walking to the kitchen.

I still stand in the same spot, in disbelief. "How did they die?"

"A teenager, texting and driving…all three lives lost in a moment."

She gets up and walks to me quickly. We hug before she allows herself to cry. Her frame is so small that I'm mindful not to squeeze her tight.

"When did it happen?" I ask her.

"Two days ago," Nia answers after a sniffle.

I wasn't even in the country yet and she has been alone since then. "I'm sorry I didn't check on you sooner."

"The funeral is tomorrow, come with me, ok?"

I'm in shock, but the memories of the past are still fresh in my mind. They are always fresh in my mind. "I'm sorry Nia, but you know I can't do that."

She moves her head away and stares at me angrily, it's hard for me to look back at her. "What did you say?"

"You can stay as long as you need to but you know why I can't go."

"Let go of me."

"Nia, I'm sorry."

"Let go of me!" When I do she takes a step away from me. "I'm going to be on your case all day, all night, non-stop, just you and me, until you come to your senses." She snaps her fingers.

Urola, awaken from her sleep I imagine, stands up on my couch and barks at Nia, shaking her little tail.

"No!" Tanya orders as she returns to the dining room, putting a tea cup and saucer on the table.

I watch Urola sit in place with a slight whimper, looking at me for help. No such luck. "Nia. What about work and your bills?" Nia gives me a look, she has a right to. I want to change the topic. "I just want to make sure if I need to put money aside for you."

"I got a substitute teacher to cover for my fifth graders and I'm taking personal time off and vacation time off to mourn."

"You're mad at me because I worry about bill collectors calling you?" My eyebrows tighten and I think I might get a headache. I'm just upset that she sees through my obvious lie as she rolls her eyes at me.

Nia answers, "My bills are on auto-pay with my credit cards. Like I said, it's just going to be you and me tonight." Nia walks back to the table and sits down with a thud, for someone her size she sure knows how to make a lot of noise when she wants to. I think she's trying to tell me that she's upset with me, no surprise there.

"DeAndre, sit," Tanya says as she sits down, tapping the chair next to her. "I let her in. I think maybe…you talk…"

"I don't want to talk, I need a real drink." I walk towards the kitchen.

"Listen to your girlfriend, DeAndre!"

"Oh…I'm not his girlfriend," Tanya quickly corrects.

"What now?" Nia asks.

I wince. I know what's coming. "She said she's not my girlfriend, Nia." I grab a glass and bottle of sweet red wine from the cabinet. I open the bottle and fill the glass to the top. I take a glance to my left and I see that the paper package of movies is next to the dishes. I can tell from the new wrinkles on the bag that she knows what is inside.

"I get it. You two are dating, seeing each other…whatever. I'm not a complete prude." Nia adds.

"I…visit," Tanya corrects, trying to find the right words, I assume.

"Excuse me?" Nia asks.

I wince again. I don't want to look back at Nia as I imagine her judging eyes are already burning a hole in the back of my head. "Here we go." I take a drink.

"You visit doing what?"

"Well…"

"Well what?" I hear Nia snap back.

"Um…DeAndre, I think…she's joking, yeah?"

I drink most of the wine and turn to Tanya. She's looking at me with a confused look and an awkward smile. "I'm so glad you opened the door for her."

"Is she a whore?" Nia asks.

I watch Tanya turn to her with a raised eyebrow. I see she finally understands who she's been talking to. "Escort," Tanya corrects.

"Oh, there's a difference? Oh wow, that amazing whore."

"Nia, stop," I reply. When Tanya raises her hand briefly to stop me from defending her, it only makes me nervous.

"I think you see me looking for man in shining armor…don't."

"Aren't you?" Nia quickly asks.

"When you survive the streets of Petersburg, then you can understand me, child."

"I am a woman, honey. Something you'll never be."

I add, "To be fair, Nia, an escort doesn't always have sex. Many lonely people are looking for attention or company…"

Nia replies to me, "Shut up, DeAndre! Sounding like an ad, damn!"

Tanya says, looking Nia up and down in a way which makes me even more nervous, "Look at you…wearing design clothes, some fancy green sweater…"

"It's called a cardigan."

"You are like some Miss Princess."

"Because that's where my name came from, Nubian princess. Ok?"

"What?"

"Speak English much, whore?"

Tanya stands up, knocking her chair back as she rolls her hands into tight fists. Nia, true to her temper, does the same. Urola barks at them both, but remains in a sitting position; this is just entertainment to Urola, but it is a bad situation for me.

"Do something! Show me what you know from being in Mother Russia." Nia pokes at Tanya's forehead with her pointer finger. "Or is laying on your back the only thing you…"

True to Tanya's form, she pulls Nia's hand away, holds and tugs at Nia's hair, and screams when Nia does the same. I put the glass and bottle down. I run to the dining room as Nia's face is planted on the table, but both are screaming from anger and pain.

"Get this bitch off me," Nia yells at me.

"Let her go," I yell at Tanya.

"First she says 'sorry,' then I let go."

Knowing my sister, that isn't going to happen. I break their hold and push them away from each other. Nia tries to make a leaping charge at Tanya but I catch her in mid-air and put her over my shoulder like a heavy bag of potatoes. I carry Nia towards the guest room.

"I'm going to get you, bitch! You should have stayed in Russia!"

"That's very Christian of you, Nia," I comment.

"You're dead, bitch!" Nia yells.

"Stay away from me, little bird, or I'll break your wings."

I turn and look back at Tanya the same way she looks at Urola when she chews on a new pair of her shoes that I've bought. Tanya crosses her arms and rolls her eyes. "Excuse me?"

"I…didn't mean that. Sorry."

"What! What did that whore-bitch say?"

"She said that you two will talk things out after you both cool down…because no one is going to do anything to each other. Understood?"

"Oh…so you're going to put your whore in front of your family?"

"Do we understand each other?" I ask as I shake Nia, a reminder of her current reality.

"Let go of me!" She slaps my back to remind me of her stubbornness, the family trait. And the thought makes my stomach turn. I put her down because of it.

She slaps my face and chest a few times before she stomps into the guest room and slams the door in my face. "Kiss my ass!"

"Is that what Jesus meant when he said something about turning the other cheek?" I smile, even when I hear her door lock.

Leaving Nia to brood, I walk towards the couch as I see Tanya sitting with Urola lying on her lap, taking deep breaths as she rubs Urola's fur. I sit down next to her and wrap my arm around her shoulder. She rests her head on my chest as we look out the view from my window, it is beautiful. The pigeons haven't stained my windows yet, the sun is shining over nearby buildings, and Central Park in the distance is set against a nice orange hue.

I hear Nia unlock the door and open it. "Jesus also said to honor your parents!"

"Actually that was God who first said it," I reply.

As Nia slams the door with an angry yell, Urola stands up and barks towards the guest room. Urola is getting a full show tonight.

"I can't believe you let her in."

"I see a little girl at the door and..."

"She's twenty-four, by the way."

"No," she says as her head pops up to look at me. I'm assuming that she's making sure that I'm not lying.

"She has good skin from our mother. But wait, in your mind, you were twisting the hair of a little girl?"

"Yes…and not her arm." Tanya pets Urola's head until the barking stops, but Urola keeps looking towards the guest room.

"I'm just saying…she's my sister, ok?"

Tanya takes a deep breath. "Tell me what you want me to do."

"Try to get along with her without fighting."

I turn my head as Nia opens her door and stomps into the kitchen. Urola barks at her until Tanya shushes her. I watch as Nia opens the fridge, mumbling loudly.

"See anything to your liking?" I ask Nia.

"What the hell is this healthy shit? Carrots and white chicken bites in bags?"

"You can order a pizza," I suggest.

I watch as she takes a bottle of water and my turkey and cheese sandwich that I was keeping for later. After she slams the fridge shut, she stomps toward the guest room. Urola wiggles free from Tanya's hold, jumps off the couch, and runs towards Nia. Not to my surprise, Nia makes kissing sounds at Urola.

What better way to get into someone's good graces or to get under their skin than by befriending their own pet? That's what Nia taught me before her French bulldog, Jack, died a few years ago.

"Come on, girl…come on," Nia says nicely to Urola.

I watch as Urola leaves us and follows Nia without looking back. "Urola is falling for Nia's pretty face and sweet sounding voice. It's just a physical thing, don't worry," I tease before Tanya elbows my side.

After Urola runs into the room, but before Nia closes the door, Tanya says, "Hey, Nia…" I watch as Nia looks at Tanya, her eyes dead set on murder if the wrong words are said. Tanya continues, turning to Nia, "Nice shoes." Nia gives her the ok sign. Tanya quickly looks at me and asks, "Does she know…?"

Nia says, "Yeah, I just looked it up Russian insults online, bitch." She slams the door, Urola barks are muffled behind the door.

"I know she's your sister…"

"Tanya, I know." I look at Tanya as she bites her lip. "But remember, what would Jesus do?"

"Not have sex for forty days."

"That's not what I heard," I reply giving her a wink.

"No, that's not the truth," she says, smiling at me.

"Jesus was a pimp."

She pinches me at my side. "Hey, be respectful."

"I'm just kidding."

"Um hmm." She rests her head on my shoulder.

"You never told me you were religious."

"I'm not…I just have enough things against me."

"Mysterious…that's so sexy. Hey, to change the subject, don't you want to know what my name means?"

"Ok."

I ignore the indifference in her voice. "I'm named after my father's police partner he lost on duty."

She kisses my cheek and holds my hand. "That's sad."

I want to laugh at her reaction, I have no illusion behind the meaning behind my name but I don't have the same emotional attachment as my father did; it became another reason for him to be disappointed in me. "I've always wanted to know the meaning behind your name."

"Whatever I want," she says simply, but her eyes looking away for a moment tells me that she's hiding internal scars neither she nor I want to get into.

We look out the window in each other's comfort. There is no need or interest to dig into each other's lives any further, because we don't need to. Ignorance is just fine with us.

THE NEXT morning, I wake up to an empty bed and the sound of modern Russian rap music playing on my entertainment system in my living room; I'm grateful that Tanya doesn't know how to use the surround sound yet. I check the time on my cell phone and it's about ten o'clock.

I step out of my bedroom and Tanya is the first sight I see. She makes an impression as she dances in the kitchen in a low cut white top, pink cotton pajamas, and white socks. She's poetry in motion. I stare at her assets, like the pervert that I am, until she turns at me, smiles, and briefly waves at me. I see that her chin looks normal.

"You look great," I comment but she looks at me with confusion on her face. "You're perfect!"

"I know," Tanya replies before she turns around, continuing to dance to the music, and preparing breakfast, I hope.

On my way to the bathroom, I sense Nia's presence by the noises she's making behind her room door. I smile as I hear Urola's barks adding to the chaos of noise inside her room. They became fast friends overnight it seems. Frankly, I don't care if it means Nia will be cleaning up Urola's messes.

I knock on her door. "Good morning!"

I get no response other than Urola's barking when I hear her run to the door. I go to the bathroom and close the door behind me to go through my usual routine. Looking at the disarray of my bathroom is heartbreaking, especially as I look for my towel. My highlight moment is being able to find my toothbrush and paste after looking through the combs, brushes, sprays, and bottles of lotions that Tanya and Nia owns.

The instant I step out of the bathroom, I smell butter in the air. Walking pass the dining room table, I confirm that the smell is coming from a freshly cut loaf of white bread with yellow butter thinly spread over the slices. The presentation is so neat that even the crumbs are spread evenly in the bread basket. I want to partake, but I want to kiss the chief first, so I only take a quick sip from one of the glasses of ice water on the table.

I walk into the kitchen and she stops dancing as she starts to chop something up. I see an open bag of walnuts and orange peels next to her. When I position myself behind her soft body there's no surprise to me that she's thoroughly cutting up a salad into even strands. So, being the gentleman that I am, I decide to invade the curves of her hips with my hands while she's occupied.

"Stop it." She recoils until I wrap my arms around her waist; resistance is futile.

"I'm just checking out the merchandise."

"Um hmm," she mutters as she puts the lettuce in a strainer and rinses it under the faucet of the sink.

I kiss her neck and the smell of her scented strawberry body lotion draws me back in for another kiss. I take a good look at her cleavage, a free preview of what is to come later.

"You can act cold, but I know you're fighting the tingling butterflies in your stomach."

"Sure, sure," she says before she bumps me away with her hips.

I stand next to her as she starts washing the peeled oranges in front of her. "If it helps my situation, I did get some new movies for you when I was out." As she turns around and grins at me, I push my luck. "So, can I kiss you now?"

"It is possible," Tanya replies with a sly smile.

"Is it possible right now?"

I smile as she kisses me on both cheeks before kissing me on the lips. All is well. Then as I hear Nia opening the door and Urola's barking getting louder, I sigh. I can't look at Nia, I'm afraid that she might upset me, I might upset her, or we'll upset each other.

"Oh I see. You can spend time with her but not with me, your only sister? Is that how it is, DeAndre, really," Nia yells at me.

"I did say good morning, Nia," I reply.

"What?"

"I said good morning!"

"Whatever! What the hell is this music playing anyway?"

As Nia walks into the bathroom and slams the door closed behind her, I look on as Urola waits in front of the bathroom door. I imagine Urola is anxious to see what other entertaining thing Nia will do next.

As I place my head on Tanya's shoulder and sigh heavily, Tanya asks, "You ok?"

I consider my line of vision before I answer. "Are you wearing a bra?" She extends her shirt outward and I forget about my problems for a moment. "Thank you."

She snaps her shirt back and kisses the top of my head. "Later, we eat."

After Tanya playfully pushes me away, I leave her alone to do her work. I turn the music down, thankfully with no complaints from Tanya, and sit at the head of the dining room table. I grab the smallest slice of bread and eat it. I'm glad it's fresh; flossing hard bits of crust out from between my teeth will only take away my time from kissing Tanya.

Two minutes later, the bathroom door opens. I turn around and look at Nia as she steps out. She's in all black; from her hat, designer sunglasses, short sleeve knee long dress, silk socks, leather heels, and her small purse full tissues with some spilling out from the top. I can't avoid Nia any longer, I ran out of excuses yesterday.

As Nia walks right towards me, Urola is following her with an outwardly blind loyalty. As Nia stands so close in front of me, I can smell her French perfume and powder scent deodorant, I hold her hand and she graciously allows it, her grip more firm than loving. This is the same girl I use to watch morning cartoons with and now she's about to do what I can't.

"Are you coming?" Nia asks me.

I can see her eyes stare right at me even with her sunglasses on. I'm actually glad her sunglasses are on because they lessen the guilt her eyes can impose on me. "I'm in my t-shirt and boxers."

"I can wait," she quickly answers.

I look down as she holds my hand with both her hands, the sentiment is moving so I ignore the fact that her purse is pressing against my fingers. I can't look at her as I answer her as rigid as I can without sounding too cold, "I'm sorry."

"They were our parents," Nia comments, her voice cracking.

"Disowning your child has its after affects."

She throws my hand away like garbage and puts her righteous point finger in my face. "Don't you dare start with that shit, not today!" She almost starts to whimper.

Urola starts barking until Tanya shushes her with one command spoken in Russian. I look up at Nia's face and I see tears tickle down her eyes. I reach out to hug her, while sitting down I can still hug most of her body. But as I do she stops me by slapping my face, no surprise there. As she dries her face with a tissue, I calm myself as a yelling match is pointless at this point.

I like Tanya's timing as she brings over the bowl of lettuce layered with orange slices and walnut pieces and places it next to me. Then she stands behind me and rubs my shoulders with her skillful hands.

I listen as Tanya says with a level of respect befitting a moment like this, "I wish you many, um, best wishes."

Nia snaps back at Tanya, "Shut up whore! And put a real damn shirt on!" Nia walks towards the front door and Urola follows. Nia yells at Urola, "Sit!"

I watch as Urola obeys immediately before Nia slams the door behind her, an action I picture her doing often while she's still staying over here.

Chapter 4: A Funeral to Avoid

FOLLOWING Tanya's suggestion to go out and clear my head, I decide to follow through with a mental note to see my good friend Miguel. I survive the long commute into South Ozone Park, Queens, listening to mostly sport talk shows on the radio and observing new additions to the city. The most notable being the Citi Bike sharing stations, I make a mental note to take a look at the website for deals or discounts; anything to save on gas.

I park in front of the Daily Bubbles car wash. The memories of working here when I was a kid are rushing at me all at once. But I can't believe it's more modern now with a lively blue and white paint job on the building. It is pretty impressive for a car wash in this area. Latin music is playing on the outdoor speakers from a local station; it helps cover the sounds of passing cars on the Southern Parkway.

I walk out my car and lock it. I'm glad I left my shades on because the glares from the two lines of drivers waiting in line would blind me otherwise. The shorter line is in front of the drive-through wash lane. The longer line is waiting in front of the hand wash lane.

Two kids on a scooter ride off the street and whizz by me on the sidewalk. I watch them to make sure they don't hit my car. After they pass my car, leaving it unmarked, I notice two thin Spanish women with brown braids, looking good in jean shorts, walking across the street. I whistle at them for fun. They don't give me a second glance; I guess I'm just one of many guys today that will get that same treatment.

Walking to the front doors, I put my glasses off. I'm about walk through the front doors and into the office building, but I stop when I see people get out of their cars from the hand wash line with cameras in their hands and grins on their faces. I follow them and see a car being cleaned by two women in wet t-shirts with the bubble company logo, blue short shorts, and white sneakers.

"Praise Jesus." I have found my religion again.

A Spanish woman with long, black hair catches my eye first. Her plump backside makes her shorts look like a g-string. The other woman is tall, white—although a little tanned from the sun—and has curly blonde hair. Her features are small but perky.

I notice that they are doing a better job taking pictures with their sponges and with each other than washing cars. At best the dirt is being replaced by dirty water marks and smudges from the old towels being used to dry the cars. I think every car will have to be cleaned again later. Not that I think any of the male or female customers taking pictures are even thinking about that now. And from the length of the line, I guess waiting means you have no family to explain yourself to.

I catch the Spanish woman crossing her legs as she bends down to wet her sponge in the water bucket. Normally a great photo shot for my camera phone, but it makes me recognize her and her friend.

"Is that Angel and Cinnamon?" I ask myself loudly, making a few guys turn to me with grins and shake their heads in confirmation before turning their attention back to Angel and Cinnamon so they can study features that only a stripper lifestyle can warrant; that's what I'm doing.

The more I stare at Angel and Cinnamon the more I relive memories from the Fallen Gentlemen's Club, not the best topless club in Jamaica, Queens, but for whoever works at the car wash it's a short driving distance; especially on pay day.

"They don't use their stage names here, playboy."

I turn around and look at Miguel, then at his thinning black hair with white hair around like sprinkles on an ice cream cone, a wrinkled button-down shirt barely covering his beer belly, and old jean pants. Six months ago he was a stud—an aging, seven foot, Latino stud, but still a stud. He's my best friend, but I have to stop myself from calling him Mr. Lopez.

We exchange a fist bump and share a bro hug with a double back tap combo. "Miguel…what happened? I left you alone for six months, man. Come on!"

He laughs briefly in his deep voice. "I know I'm like the old man used to be. I keep to the office, deal with employee issues, time cards for payroll, taxes…"

I yawn and stretch my arms for effect. "Yeah, that's so interesting."

"Yeah, yeah…what's up?"

I walk to his side, turn around, and point to Angel and Cinnamon. "What's up with this?"

He grins. "It's their idea and my favorite time of the day."

I watch him as he stares with lustful focus at the ladies. "So…ah, which one are you crushing on, Angel or Cinnamon?"

"They work for me man, that's it."

"Right, because you have to keep things professional with strippers washing cars." I wink at him.

"It's not like that bro."

"What is it like then? I know, on slow days you get back massages, lord knows you need both of them for those enormous shoulders of yours. Wait is that lip gloss on your collar?"

"Cut that shit out." Miguel swats my inspecting hand away from his neck, but it doesn't stop him from smiling a big silly grin. "So how you've been, man?" He asks without breaking his stare on the women. I am not mad at him for his lack of focus towards me, taking a quick look at Cinnamon's massive distractions moving back and forth in her shorts makes me speechless. Miguel jokes, "Really, that's interesting, tell me more."

"What, oh yeah," I answer as I model my black suit a little, remembering that it's Armani and deserves a little vogue. "What, no props?" I turn in place.

He laughs, finally looking at me. "Still the playboy at your age?"

"Hey, man, don't hate, appreciate. And don't think I'm going to let you change the topic without answering my question about which washer is your favorite."

"You know it was my birthday last week, right?"

He hits me with the bit of knowledge that makes me realize that my mind is no longer a steel trap of information, although his memory has always been better than mine. "Will money for the strip club suffice?" He quickly puts his hands out. "Both hands," I question.

"Money is tight in this economy," Miguel replies.

I generously give him a few hundred dollar bills and several twenties, a total of five hundred and forty dollars; enough for him to have a good time at the strip club for a night. I cross my arms and sigh as Miguel starts counting the cash in front of me. "Do you need a minute?"

"Why, are you going to give me more money?"

"Keep hope alive, my brother from another mother. Keep hope alive."

I'M GIVEN a tour inside the Daily Bubbles office building with Miguel sharing the improvements he's made with the building's wiring, installation, and some of the staff. But he continues to ask me what I'm really doing visiting him out of the blue, especially after I make excuse after excuse. I tell him eventually that I'm just avoiding going to my parents' funeral. It cuts the tour short and he leads me into his office.

As we walk into his office, he immediately sits down on his chair and starts looking through the paperwork on his desk. I smell strawberry body spray that a woman would leave behind, I would tease him about it but from his body language it seems that I've already upset him. I sit down in his guest chair, worrying for a moment as the wood creaks.

"So, are you mad about not getting the invite," I ask, waiting to hear a confirmation of the obvious. "I just found out yesterday, so…"

"Don't," he utters as gives me a brief narrowed look before returning to his paperwork.

I smile. I'm getting flashbacks of when I was in trouble with his father for getting into fights at work. Mr. Lopez was always tough but fair, but tougher when it came with Miguel. All Miguel needs are glasses and a bald spot and the transformation is complete. Although, buying him a modern black shirt and new khaki pants might save him from that fate.

"Nia will be fine. Friends of the family will be there." I watch on as he just ignores me. That hasn't stopped me for the past fifteen years and it won't stop me now. "So do you have any words of wisdom, my brother from another mother?"

"DeAndre," Miguel says after a deep sigh.

"Yeah," I reply, matching his tone.

"Come soft to the playground and you go home like Mr. Softee."

"What the…" I see him smile as he signs several pages of paper. "Oh, you got jokes now?"

"You know you shouldn't be here, right?" Miguel asks.

"I thought you would need the company," I reply with a smile.

"Yeah, me too, that's why we're here," Miguel replies as he goes into his right drawer, taking out two medium-sized glasses and a half empty bottle of whiskey. I smile. It was the same thing he did when I visited him after he'd lost his mother in his arms when she died from a heart attack and his father died in a hit and run accident a few years later; the only good thing from Miguel's loss was it gave him motivation get out and kept out the gang life. "No speeches or memories…" Miguel begins to say.

"Just drinks," I reply. He's still the same rock. He's my idol.

Miguel quickly adds, "But you're still an asshole for being here instead of being with Nia at the funeral."

I smile as he puts the glasses on the desk and slowly pours whiskey evenly into them. I take a glass, he takes the other, we clink glasses, and we take a drink. Miguel leans back in his chair with a sigh. I keep my smile. I need to; I forced myself to stop crying when I left home when I was a kid.

"Since I'm an emotional mess, do you think I can get any of that money back," I ask.

"Not on your life," Miguel answers.

We laugh a good laugh. I need more of that.

Chapter 5: Consciences

OF ALL THE places I never thought I'd be in my life, the Butterfly Club in Morningside Heights hits the top three. But according to Tanya, this is the place that Nia says she will be after going to the funeral. That means that she's still emotional. That means she's going to do something stupid that might get her into trouble; I'm not ok with that.

It took a hundred bucks just to skip the line even though I look as smooth as I normally do in a suit and tie. But as I look around inside I understand why—everyone has to be under twenty-five in casual clothes. And where else would they be on a Saturday night? The butterflies in stomach must be my conscious calling me a pervert for just being here.

I look through the large group of friends crowding on couches to my left telling stories, while girls are grinding on who are, I assume, their boyfriends with football jackets on. Otherwise, they are taking pictures of each other on their cell phones, making funny faces.

I cringe to the high-pitched sounds of young men and women screaming as the white ceiling lights change into neon purple lights and dubstep music plays with loud drumbeats, distorted synthesizer sounds, and crazy robot vocals. My ears are being violated in immeasurable ways. I'm in hell.

I only know what this crap is because Nia played some on her cell phone a few times during our Thanksgiving dinner at a Chinese restaurant two years back. But a tight click of five women in cotton shirts, short jeans, and flip flops run pass me and unto the dance floor, showing me they think otherwise of the music. They look goofy as they fail at twerking, but they are having fun. I'm deducing from this access of released energy that mid-year exams are done and everyone wants to forget their troubles. It's no wonder Nia is somewhere in this playhouse.

I suddenly spot her getting hit on by a young punk that looks as stupid as he dresses; he reminds of me at his age. I walk to them and see Nia notices me first, and it doesn't bother me that her smile lessens; I expect that and more from her tonight. I tap on her suitor's shoulder and give him a terrifying look when he turns to me, but I also have a fifty showing between my fingers.

"Hey, make this easy on yourself and impress another girl by buying her a drink."

He sizes me up and stands up straight; I'm still five inches taller and bigger than he is. He takes the money and leaves. Smart, he definitely reminds me of myself at that age. I look Nia over as she looks away, as if the sight of me sickens her. But I still am able to see that her makeup is done up, though not so much in the area around her eyes. Her hair is in some kind of fancy ponytail to accent her strapless dress that is short and inappropriate—Nia, true to form.

"What you doing here, Nia?" She turns to me and tries to punch me in my stomach, but I block it. She has no speed and muscle behind it. "Yo!"

"Don't talk to me, I...hate...you...leave me...alone," she slurs.

I look around. "And this is where you decide to grieve?"

"Better than...you," she says, moving her head side to side with attitude.

"You're done here." I go to grab her arm, but she swats my hand away.

She stands up and digs her pointer finger into my chest before she yells, "You don't...get..."

I look into her glazed eyes before she blinks hard and tears up. I would normally look down in shame if I didn't smell some kind of kiwi-flavored drink on her breath. I would ask her if getting drunk is a good idea, but she could ask me the same question about the whiskey on my breath.

"Listen..."

"No!"

She pushes me away and I watch her walk onto the dance floor. I'll let her make a fool of herself to appease whatever demons she has inside; I owe her that much. As she becomes one with the collective, I'm in awe that despite her lack of motor skills she is dancing as well as everyone else.

She's no artist on the dance floor, but she's relishing the sounds of loud screams as she jumps up and down, clapping perfectly to the rhythm to the music. I can't believe, in her condition, that she has enough control of her body to spin around in place and not throw up, and so do the guys around her. I watch them and their hands.

There are a few guys that try to approach her, but they can't keep up with her pace and laugh away their shame as they walk away. But then there is a tall man that moves people away harshly and then holds Nia in place to make her stop jumping. He tries to force a kiss, but she slaps him on his face and it only makes him laugh. As the crowd parts, his face is clearly shown. I can't believe the world is this small.

"Frankie."

I'm already moving through the crowd before my brain can come up with an excuse or lie good enough to stop Frankie. His wide grin as he manhandles her enrages me. He can mess with me but not with her, never her. Nia slaps him rapidly and no one is stupid enough to do anything about it except for me.

I swing at him and I partially hope I miss, but I don't. I hardly ever do when I aim at a target. Before I calculate how much shit I'm in, I see the shock in Frankie's face as my fist hits the side of his jaw. Nia almost follows him to the floor from the momentum until I catch her.

I yell, "Let's get out of here!"

My heroics are cut short as a crushing grip from a large, white hand wraps around my throat. The grip is from a working man, a strong man. So I don't even have see Tony's face behind me to know it is him, but I check to confirm. Then gravity stops applying to me as Tony lifts me up and cuts off my air supply.

I kick and punch at his pudgy body for a few seconds before my field of vision starts to become a field of white dots. I see Frankie get up and get a few punches into my stomach before Tony points out the crowd starting to record everything on their cell phones.

Frankie says something to me but sound is replaced by a loud hum in my ears and my vision is almost completely white before Tony lets me go. Nia runs to my side as I gasp for air, watching Frankie and Tony walk away. I see that the crowd turns off their cell phones as Frankie gives them a look that would scare any drug addict straight.

As my breathing goes back to normal, I can hear Nia yell, "Bro! Are you alright?"

I don't know what to say. I just look around at the crowd of curious people surrounding us. I know what's coming next. I didn't hear what Frankie's words were, but you don't touch a man like Frankie without it costing you. I'm going to be made an example of if I don't think fast about how I'm going to prevent that from happening.

"HE DID WHAT?"

These are the last words I want to hear as I walk back into my apartment, but I see that my deed has preceded me. Tanya turns to me with wide open eyes as I assume the update continues from whomever she's talking to on her cell phone.

Nia walks past me, making sure to push me aside first, and stomps towards her room. She doesn't wait for Urola, who is running around the couch and trying to catch up to her. Nia slams and locks the door, the result of me outing myself as a hired killer during the car ride here. Urola sits and waits in front of the door after she barks once. The door unlocks and opens slightly, just enough to let Urola inside. The door slams shut again and is immediately locked.

I close and lock the door behind me. I stand against the door and wait for Tanya's mystery person to finish talking to her and for Tanya's unmoving stare to stop piercing into me. I look right back into her, awaiting my sentence.

"Yes…he just got here…ok…ok…bye."

She hangs up and I'm suddenly uncomfortable, squirming in my skin like I'm about to get ambushed. "Who was it?"

"Tony."

"What?" I stand up as if his large hand is on my throat again.

"He told me…"

"His version of the truth?"

"He saved your life."

Before I ask her why she's so defensive of him, I replay the situation and it makes sense that he's the one that stops Frankie and points to the phones the college students were using, but I'm still cautious because it also makes sense that Frankie would use Tony to get me into false sense of security. I walk to the living room windows and scan the streets for people who don't belong in the neighborhood. I don't see anyone in Frankie's crew, but they don't need to follow me. Frankie can find anyone for the right price to get the job done.

"What did Tony say?"

"That you messed up."

I scan the uncovered windows in the buildings across me—the same neighbors arguing, exercising, and watching television. "I know. But he was touching Nia…"

"You never involve, but for her you do?"

"If I didn't know any better, I'd think you were jealous." I look at the passing cars.

"I'm…disappointed."

"Save me the trouble and tell me how mad you are." I'm use to waiting, patience is a virtue in my business, but I rather just get arguments out of the way.

"Tony tells me that you and Nia can leave tonight, that's it. And I can go back."

"Just business as usual," I ask her, the window to escape I was just given is still not fully registering in light of Tanya's comment.

"What Frankie can do…is very bad. You understand it?" Tanya asks.

"Yeah, that sounds about right." I've known her for a year, collectively, but I thought there was a friendship. To see her ready to go at a drop of a hat is reality check to my pride.

A knocking on a door makes me turn around and I see Tanya is standing in front of Nia's door. "My dog please," Tanya yells through the door.

"And it's odd, that Tony knows your number."

"No, it isn't."

"Wow." My thoughts on how she's been taking care of Urola and how she bought a fur coat without me just got answered. I can see a con coming a mile away, but this is different. She is a quality professional.

"I have no words to explain for you. I just want to live." Tanya comments.

I walk to Tanya as I watch Nia open the door and hand Urola to her before slamming the door in her face. She turns around and takes a step back when she sees me already behind her. I just look at her, more from disappointment than anger.

"To customers who spoil me, I am very good. You understand?"

The word 'customers' cements my feet to the reality I forgot I put myself in. "Business…as usual." I understand why this is happening and how it has to happen, it still sucks.

Two people guarding the ghosts of their pasts weren't built for times like this. Her life path must have made her into some kind of person that survives by making sure nothing conflicts with her money. I survive by keeping people and my own feelings in neat, organized buckets, along with the burdens they came with.

For those reasons, we never really knew where we stood with each other until now. She doesn't have my back and she never will. "Be safe, Tanya."

"Keep open your eyes. Take care not to die."

"Sure." I look down, waiting for Tanya to leave. I smile as Urola licks my chin before Tanya carries her away. Urola's first and last act of kindness towards me and it's on a night like this. I would be sad, but what would be the point? It's what I wanted, easy come easy go. It's what I paid for.

I hear the front door open and close. Nia's door immediately unlocks and opens.

"Don't start," I tell her as I look up at her.

"I wasn't, I just want to give my brother a hug." Nia hugs me with a mother's warm embrace. "I'm going to miss that dog," she adds.

Chapter 6: Home Sweet Home

IT ONLY TOOK fifteen minutes after Tanya left to get packed, ten of which was spent explaining to the police officer that was called in by an upset neighbor that there was no domestic dispute, just a family argument that sounded like the same thing. As Nia packs the back seat of my car with her bare essentials, I check the trunk, the engine, and under the car for anything that doesn't belong there. We're good to go.

"What, the pot holes ruin your pretty car?"

"You got jokes now?"

"Where the hell are we going, our parent's house? They left it to me, by the way."

Of course they did. "They will look there after coming here." I look inside and make sure the back seat is perfectly balanced with our stuff without covering my view out the back window. Appeased, we both get into my car and I start it.

"How can they find it so quickly? It's not in my name yet and there is more than one Johnson family around."

"But I bet the mortgage papers being processed have your name on it."

"But how does that link…"

"And when the will becomes public record, they'll find both our names…get it?"

"You got a few old boxes and photo albums, by the way." I look at her and sigh as she casually buckles up. "What?"

"We need to hide this car, switch the E-Z Pass to Miguel's black Chevy Silverado, lay low, and wait for the backup I just called in to come in a few days."

"Wait...Miguel's truck? Where are we going? Where else can we stay for few days other than a hotel that's safe?"

Now I have to tell her that I want to involve Miguel, the same person she's helping join the Boys and Girls club; as I found out from my talk with Miguel. "We're going to a safe place in Queens."

"Hey, buckle up."

"No!" I merge into traffic, gleefully out of spite.

"Queens? Isn't that, like, thirty minutes from here? Where are we going exactly that can't be found with a GPS?"

"Woodhaven. Frankie doesn't have influence there anymore and he would need to get permission to do anything there. And permission takes time."

"Sometimes your business is slow, poor you."

I wish I was in the mindset to argue with her right now, but I have to stay focused. "Let's just stick with the matter at hand. Miguel will..."

"I don't think you should get Miguel involved in your mess."

Here we go, she's in defense mode. "The O.G.s from the LCF works at his car wash because they're on the Project Clean Slate like him. They owe him. We'll be safe under his protection." I didn't think recognizing the LCF tattoos on Miguel's staff would become useful information, but life is funny. Latin Crew Forever, that brings back all kinds of promiscuous memories.

"Didn't you tell me you were some bad ass? Why do you need Miguel?"

"The difference between a bad ass and a professional is that a professional knows when to go to get help." My mind briefly pictures Tanya for a moment.

"Ok, Mr. Professional, what does a bad ass do?"

The barrage of bullets that hits my back window answers her question. She yells as I speed through traffic.

"It's alright! The windows and insulation in the car are bullet proof!"

"It's not alright! Get me the hell out of here!"

I see a silver Ford MKZ racing behind us in my rear view mirror. "Oh...is that the new model?" I focus on the road immediately after it hits my back bumper and another barrage of bullets hit and start to crack my back window.

"Shit, shit, shit...I thought you said the windows were bullet proof," Nia yells.

"Get down!" I lower her by her head until she sinks into the seat.

Frankie must have been on Tony's ass to push the order through. Now someone is trying to look good by getting an early paycheck. That is just my luck tonight. I cut through more traffic, carefully bobbing and weaving past several minivans. I watch as the MKZ does the same, but it nearly hits a few people walking on the sidewalk as we speed past by.

I've got to lose him. I push the accelerator to the floor and my side mirrors shake like I am in a racecar. I quickly spot Nia pressing an imaginary brake. "What the hell are you doing?

"What are you doing? This isn't NASCAR 2013!"

I look at the driver's side view mirror for a moment before it gets shot off. "My mirror! Oh, that's it!"

I spin around into a parking building as Nia screams, "You're driving like a maniac!"

The MKZ trails behind, losing control as it hits the sidewall while I speed up the spiral driveway. As soon as I reach the top, I take a hard left and Nia screams again. My attention is sharp and nerves are super responsive as I spin the car around, putting my seat belt on.

I race towards the entry as the MKZ speeds out. I crash into the driver's side and pin the car to the wall. My front window cracks, but the back seat is covered with shattered glass from the rear window.

"Oh yeah, got you!"

"Holy…shit."

"Are you ok?" I look her over and she's shaking, but she's unmarked. "You're fine."

I get out of the car and my age catches up to me as I groan at my backaches. I look over my car and it looks like Swiss cheese married a strainer. I walk to the other car and I'm amazed that there's a mini-gun mounted on the dashboard. I admire how the shells are feed from and vacuumed back into an ammunition box in the back seat via a tube system.

I walk to the driver seat and am surprised to see who it is. It actually makes me smile. "Pee Pants?"

He mumbles Italian slurs at me, but he's pinned by his door and can't make a move. Besides that, the impact shattered his arm, as it looks disjoined. His head is covers in bruises and open bloody cuts. In the face of the gruesome view, he still makes me laugh for also wetting his pants. The nickname must have really spread quickly and cost him time with the ladies for him to want to be first in line to come after me. I reach for the Colt SSP handgun from his chest holster to put him out of his misery.

"No!"

I turn around and see Nia standing outside the car, looking at me and judging me. "He just tried to kill us, Nia."

"We're able to walk away, he's not. Justice is done."

"Did you just say…justice?"

"The police will be coming soon, come on!"

I roll my eyes and the turn to Pee Pants. "Good luck with Frankie."

MIGUEL'S PLACE has the same white paint on his house since I moved out and the metal security screen door stills grinds when I open it. His window still has a hole from a bullet that hit it last year, an attempted robbery that got scared away; no other attempts were made that year. I do notice the new addition of a security camera above the door.

I knock on Miguel's door and it takes a moment before I hear his large footsteps coming to the door.

"You sure they didn't follow us?" Nia asks.

"I think we're safe from the maids from the dollar van."

After dumping my car in an abandoned parking lot, it was with cautious optimism that we took a dollar van instead of a city bus. There is no way anyone in Frankie's circle rides in dollar vans. They wouldn't be caught dead in a van that needs a rope to open and close the door and a driver watching out for the TLC police.

Miguel opens the door, looking at us briefly and then at our bags on the ground covered in leaves and sticks. "What happened?" He asks.

"There's a hit out on me and I need a place to stay low until my back-up from Africa arrives. In the meanwhile, I need you and the O.G.s to cover our asses. And I need my car to be picked up and taken to the nearest chop shop."

He takes a moment and then replies, "Ok."

He takes Nia's bags and leads us inside.

"That's it? Are you sure it's ok, Miguel?" Nia asks.

"Get your butt inside," I order her.

"Don't tell me what to do," she quickly replies, pointing her finger at me before storming inside.

"Jesus, are you my sister or our mother?" I reply before I pick up my bags and walk inside.

Miguel closes the door and locks it. He picks up the same bags and walks downstairs with them. Nia follows him after he turns on the lights with his elbow. I look around the place and Miguel hasn't changed anything in it, my home away from home. The fade on the blue carpet and the wires on the television dangling off the wall are history marks from boyhood foolery. And the picture of the Latin Jesus is still framed on the wall.

There is an unopened bag of snack mix on the living room table and a Chinese menu with the receipt still on it in the garbage bin, glad to see Miguel has kept up with his eating habits. It still smells like what he cooked an hour ago, pasta from what I can guess, and it's driving me crazy. I follow them to the basement before I raid his fridge. The stairs creak when I step on them and I imagine they scream when Miguel stomps on them.

I look out the basement's windows as I drop my bags down near the bottom steps. It's dirty, making the night sky look mud brown. The sounds of the passing traffic easily seep through the shut windows. I make mental notes to clean and oil them accordingly.

Miguel pats my shoulder and gives me a nod as he walks upstairs. I know what that means; the O.G.s will be on call shortly.

"His place is worse than yours," Nia comments as I watch her look over at the rusty washer, the dryer machine, and the piles of aged boxes with disgust.

I smile. "Even better, he mostly orders out and drinks soda. How do you think I picked up my eating habits?"

"At least your place had a view, but your choice in company has improved at least."

"I'm happy if you're happy."

"So, what's the plan?" Nia asks, looking at me.

"We lay low now."

"No…what's the whole plan? When do we get the police involved? Are your friends from Africa with the FBI or an anti-crime team or something?"

"No, but they are just as committed, fair enough?"

"Exactly how they are going to help us against the mob?"

"Listen, the less you know…"

"You're horrible."

I look at her and blink hard. "You'll live through it."

"How are you not affected by this? Jesus Christ, save me."

I glance at the goose bumps on her arms when she crosses them and I realize that she's not just being righteous. "We'll be fine, ok? Listen, Pee Pants…"

"This is a man we're talking about right?"

I sigh. "You're my beacon of humanity as always."

"Who else is going to worry about your ass?"

"Why me, God," I ask looking upward.

"Why? Because one of the worst things in the world is to be a human being that has no apathy," Nia answers.

Chapter 7: The Prisoner's Dilemma

"SO IS BOREDOM part of your genius master plan?"

I focus on keeping my count as I do my push-ups. I already have the heat working against me, despite the portable house fan running on high since this morning. And outside the open window, I hear women cursing at each other in English then Spanish, birds chirping non-stop, dogs barking at each other, loud horns from passing cars, and then police sirens in the far distance.

"Please let me finish," I tell her.

"How many push-ups are you doing?"

"It's my fifth set of fifty." Hearing it said out loud makes me consider doing jumping jacks.

"Is that supposed to be rewarding or keep you busy? And how can you even be touching that carpet?"

"How is the puzzle coming along?" Like I need to ask, I heard her play some game app on her phone for ten minutes after giving her the puzzle box I found in the basement to keep her busy.

"I've been Tweeting and checking Facebook on my phone."

"You need to get off, now."

I sit back, resting on my knees, and look back at Nia. The puzzle tiles are in piles in front of her, and not one piece is put together. She diligently looks through her phone, swiping her finger on the screen. I should have known better. I clear my throat until she finally looks at me.

"What'd I do now?"

"What did I say, Nia? No phones, no…"

"It's Facebook. I'm looking at my friend's picture at Gospel Fest, no one is looking…"

"Want to bet your life on it?" I watch her take a moment and hope my point is made.

"I turned off the tracking apps, give me some credit."

"When did you turn them off?"

"You're on my case but you're fine with Miguel going out to work like normal?"

"Exactly, he's going to work like normal."

"He's the only other family you got."

"He has the O.G.s, remember?"

"The O.G.s aren't you."

"If there's a problem, we'll call each other in code." I continue with my push-ups.

"If you're so concerned why don't look out the window or something?"

"I did." I count a little louder.

She continues, "You looked only once at three o'clock in the morning, then at five."

"God save me." I count a little louder and close my eyes.

"Oh! There's a special showing at the Westside Theatre on 43rd Street. Can we go there at ten o'clock?"

"Oh come on!" I lost my count and I'm losing my patience.

"Ok…ok….there's a parade on Union Square we can go to…"

"We can't go." I restart my count.

"Why?"

"It's twenty minutes away from Melrose!"

"What's in Melrose?"

"Shut up...just shut up!" I'm taken back to memories of yelling at Nia when she was six years old.

"No! I'm bored! You can't talk to me? Fine! Teach me some karate moves...teach me something!"

I sit on my knees again. I can't laugh out loud and do push-ups at the same time. "Teach you some what? Shit." I needed a good laugh.

"I'm a fast learner."

"Yeah, ok," I reply, wiping the sweat off my head.

"I'm not kidding."

"You want to learn how to kill people?"

"Defend myself." Nia is quick to correct me.

"Oh, if that's the case, then...no," I reply back.

"Listen..."

"We have a car filled with O.G.s driving around the block every hour and..."

"How does that help me?"

"Ok, I will tell you this much. Watch out for anything silver. Cars, suits, boats, whatever...if it's silver, you run in the other direction, got it?"

"Why is that?"

"Inside joke between modern assassins...it's the color of the payment that Judas got for backstabbing Jesus."

"Whatever...is the news safe to watch?"

"On television, sure it is."

"Oh my God, save me."

She goes back to her phone and I figure that I'll give her another day with it before I steal it from her. "Watch only the news, ok?"

"Oh shit…that guy from yesterday is dead."

I go back to my push-ups, ignoring the strain creeping up my arms. I knew Pee Pants was a dead man when I left him; he didn't get the job done. "What happened to him?"

"His body was found with a bullet through his chest. It wasn't even found in the parking lot but by the Harlem Meer…they're calling it a jacking gone wrong."

They take the car away and dump the body. Less questions that way, considering the wild ride through the streets last night. "That sounds about right."

"You're telling me you knew that he was going to die regardless?"

I grin, she gets it now. "That's what he gets for trying to kill us."

"What's wrong with you? You play this funny, strong man and then you say things like that."

I rest on my knees and calm my breathing. "You'll get used to it…"

"I don't want to get used to it! I want my brother back…my real brother!" She gives me her signature unapproved look, which I thought she'd be tired of doing by now.

"You don't know me."

"What? You were playing video games with Miguel at my apartment last Christmas."

"I also play with multiple passports and phones at times."

"Blah, blah, blah…got anything else to say that I haven't seen in a movie?"

I take off my shirt and show her my bare back, hoping to shut down any follow-up righteousness. "My Russian trainer gave me the name of the Vulture. It's my work badge, my work history. As you can tell from the size of the bird and the number of feathers, I'm an expert."

As I put my shirt back on she asks, "Why would you do that to yourself?"

I sigh as her expression changes from rage to disappointment. I'll never keep her quiet or happy it seems. For a moment, I miss my arrangement with Tanya. "If you're traditionally trained, you're inked…it's like a calling card that holds your reputation and work ethic."

"And what is your work ethic?"

"You don't want to go there with me." I hate showing the bad parts of myself to Nia.

"Tell me, DeAndre," Nia orders me; I'm the six year old in the room now, I get brief flashbacks of being in trouble with our mother.

"It's whatever the contract dictates, with the exception of conflicts of interest and children."

Nia sighs. "What was it like, your first contract?"

"No comment." That's one of many questions I'm going to avoid answering.

"I thought so," Nia replies with a grimace.

"So, that being said, how do you see your brother now?"

"I see you more as…"

"As what," I ask, grimly interested in hearing her thoughts on the subject.

"A sad clown."

"Why is that? I have a wonderful sister, a great friend…"

"You just lost your parents and pretend it doesn't bother you."

"It takes practice. You can become someone else when you need to by simply changing your name if you want. You can act different, be more confident, and happier. And forget that your other life ever happened."

I watch Nia take a moment. Then she replies, "Are you happy? Before this madness, you would hang out with me or Miguel a few months a year and catch up on our lives, never talking about yours. You'd visit mommy for food and fight with daddy if he was in the house. Then you leave us for the rest of year."

"No, I'd stop at strip clubs first," I joke but look down at the floor for a moment; I don't like this conversation.

"You're an idiot."

I laugh. "I know."

"I know you and daddy…"

"We're not talking about it." I grit my teeth. I wish she could leave things alone.

"I get it! And I know our parents fought and hit each other when you were growing up. But they made up! They got better! They became better people!"

I stand up and walk toward the stairs. I'm not playing her game. I'm not going to look back on my life and upbringing and share my feelings. Her small but firm hand on my arm is trying to anchor me in place; I only stop because I don't want her following me upstairs.

"Let go of me."

I don't look at her but it doesn't stop her from saying, "Our father wanted to reach out to you, but he couldn't because…"

"The Johnson pride, I know."

"Shame, asshole."

I start to shake from anxiety. "Let go of me."

"And you'll go where? Go to your hooker?"

"She's an escort." Even now I defend her honor. Damn I'm either sad or horny.

"Who cares? I'm the last pillar of support you have left big brother, one day you'll have to listen me."

"We're done here," I reply back, giving her an angry stare.

Nia only looks back at me with sad eyes. "You're better than a creature of death. The church says…"

"Oh my God…you want to talk about the church, fine! I don't care about the church. Not even as a child. I was the loud kid in church. If Mom said to be quiet, I told her to be quiet. I'd run up and down the aisle because I wasn't going to sit down for an hour. And even if our dad pinned me down, I'd just kicked the shoes of the poor soul who sat in front of me. What do you have to say to that?"

I watch as Nia starts to tear up and think I just rocked her argument, but when she laughs I'm caught off guard. As soon as she lets me go, I run up the stairs like I am being timed. Despite being at the end of my wits, I realize after I deconstruct my last comment that I just made her argument: our home life wasn't all bad.

"Whatever," I finally say as I reach the top of the steps.

"That's fine big brother, daddy's counselor had to deal with the same stubbornness. It took hitting rock bottom…"

"Just stay down here!"

"Why?"

"Just…do what I say!" I yell back, so angry I fell like throwing something.

"Why?"

"You need me to stay alive!"

"And you need me stay a good person!" Before I close the door behind me, she adds, "Get me a cup of ice water while you're up there!"

"Fine," I reply back, slamming the door shut.

IT'S A HUMID Thursday afternoon and my friends have been delayed in Africa too long for my liking. But with nothing else to do, Miguel and I are in basement working out with his dumbbells. Normally Miguel would be working, but he's letting his office vice manager run the car wash; I told him about my heart to heart conversation with Nia yesterday, so he's giving me morale support today. And thankfully, Miguel bought additional fans yesterday, so the basement is now more tolerable.

So, I make most of his time by getting him back in the mindset of eating healthy and working out. Getting my lifting buddy back takes me back to going to the gym with him, working out and shooting the shit. And having someone else to talk to other than Nia is another bonus. Nia is doing God knows what upstairs in the kitchen and the living room, but her footsteps on the floor above me are enough indication that I don't need to check on her often.

In between my sets, I keep watch of the basement window and the downstairs monitor for the new front and back camera feed. Not exactly action footage watching grass grow and cars drive by, but it gives us piece of mind.

After my next set, I look out the basement window and see the same two Spanish women I saw last week walk past Miguel's house carrying plastic grocery bags. I would think nothing of them, but there are ten guys across the street, hanging out in front of a white painted house, looking at them while calling out for sexual favors. Then these guys start to yell out demands as the women continue to ignore them; I hate bullies.

There's something in my gut that says something bad is going to happen. I watch as Miguel stands next to me and sees what I see. We exchange a look and a head nod, that's all I need.

As we run upstairs I yell, "Nia!"

"What?" she replies.

As soon as I walk into the living room, I see her putting up black rosary beads over the front door. "Stay in the house," I order.

"Nope. It's just you and me, remember?"

"But…"

"But what?" She asks, snaking her head at me. "You're not leaving me alone, with no gun, karate training, or anything."

"Just stay here!"

"I'm not a damn a dog!" Nia yells as Miguel walks pass me, takes one of his car wash's logo caps hanging on the wall by hooks like Christmas decorations, puts the cap on her head, opens the door, and walks outside. "Hey," she protests.

"I have the keys, come on," Miguel says.

It's funny watching Nia adjusting the cap to her small head. It also makes her look like a small boy; three guys look more formidable than two.

"What is this, the nineties? This is stupid," Nia says after I help her angle the cap with some style.

"You're stupid," I tease. "Just follow our lead," I tell Nia before pushing her outside and locking the door behind me.

We follow and catch up to the women. Miguel and I exchange looks with the guys across the street, measuring each other's numbers. Before I can think of anything to say Nia utters, in her normal voice, "Hey ladies, you need help?"

I don't have time to be mad at her. I can only wave at the two women as they look back at us, I just don't want them more nervous than they already are. That and I don't want a face full of mace.

But one of them looks at me with a double take and asks, "DeAndre?"

"Hey…" I say with a smile. I'm trying to figure out who she is that she can recognize me just like that.

"It's me, Tina," she says with a sudden wide smile, pointing to herself.

Her eyes trigger the memory of when I was young and had the bright idea to help a cute little girl against five boys bigger and stronger than me. These boys were bullies to most of the kids, but worst to any girls they actually liked. I fought them long enough to get the supervising teacher's attention. That was the day that I realized that I was lover not a fighter, well, unless I have help or the advantage. That was the same week when I met a big kid named Miguel.

I see her friend gauge my size with her eyes while tapping her feet and I realize I'm taking too long to answer. "Oh hey, how are you?"

"Come here, you!" She puts her groceries down and gives me a hug. We both don't care that our shirts are covered in sweat. It's entertaining to see her friend's eyes narrow; but message received, I'm not to enjoy Tina's slim figure or her features pressing against me.

"Wow, you're all grown up. And who's your friend?" I want to get the obvious out the way so that we can start walking.

Tina backs away and laughs. "That's Maria. She's my partner, silly."

"I'm sorry. I've been away. How are you, Maria?" I smile even though Maria just gives me a nod and the briefest of smiles.

"Wow, the world is small. But where have you been, man?" Tina asks.

"Around, but I'm back because my parents died recently. So, you know…"

"Oh no," Tina says, rubbing my left arm.

"Yeah, I'm just spending time with family and friends right now…this is my sister here, my homey." I'm a phony emitting a sense of sadness, but it is entertaining to watch Maria sneer at me as I get all of Tina's attention; being without Tanya's company, I'll take what I can get.

"Hey," Nia waves to acknowledge herself.

I watch as Miguel simply head nods to everyone before taking a look back; I imagine to make sure the guys on the other end stays there, which they do when I take a peak. If it wasn't Miguel's size, it was his connection to the LCF that kept them in place.

"Yeah, I understand." Tina takes my hand, getting my attention back, and pats my hand. "Be strong," she says with a sympathic smile.

"I will," I reply.

"Hey! I'm cooking tonight, pork with brown rice and beans. And then I'm going to make some white peach sangria after that. Come over. We can talk and maybe tomorrow I can make something special. Is that alright?" Tina asks.

"Well, I don't want to impose." I want to see how serious this sudden invite is.

"Tell me you're coming, I refuse to accept no as answer," Tina comments, stomping her foot on the ground.

I give a look to Nia and she shrugs her shoulders. I turn to Miguel and he grabs her bags in his hands; I'll take that as a yes.

"I guess we're coming," I answer before we share a laugh, Maria's surprised look is enjoyable to look at as Tina walks to my side, wraps her arm around mine, and we walk forward.

As we walk, Tina immediately talks about her life after elementary school and laughs at funny moments of her life like we were long time girlfriends. And in that moment she admits to me in a whisper that she is having a fight with Maria, who still remains silent for reasons unknown to me. It must be a serious argument.

I look back briefly at Maria, nothing silver on her; no silver clothing, hair clips, fingernails, shoes, eye color, or make-up. Then I notice that Maria and Nia are looking back at me with the same look of disapproval; I foresee them both becoming fast friends at the dinner table. My only worry is that Nia might say something she shouldn't, so I wonder how many kicks under the table I will have to share with her before she gets the clue.

Miguel is trailing behind us all, but I can tell that the thought of home cooking and a sweet Spanish drink is motivating him forward as he licks his lips. I make a mental note to buy him an exercise machine and to get him into watching cooking shows.

Chapter 8: Veil Threats

TGIF, MY ass. I swear the days are getting longer and longer. Friday is no different, than yesterday, or Wednesday; with the exception of Tina's company yesterday. But I am back to my routine. I've done mostly exercise after breakfast; a hundred jumping jacks, eighty knee highs, and ninety mountain climbers. I check my watch and it's nine in the morning; I would be bored to tears, but I'm too weak to cry.

Nia has finally decided to do some cleaning, because talking to me leads to arguments and forced Miguel back to work; you can complain to Miguel for so long before he walks away.

Seeing no other option, I take a long shower in Miguel's tub. The process, though, is still something I have to get use to. I have to keep my feet close together when standing in the tub and readjust the showerhead to its maximum angle so the water can reach my chest. I can only imagine the comedy of errors that Miguel goes through.

After my shower, I change into a pair of old exercise clothes and black sneakers that I packed. Now, the only thing I'm looking forward to is Tina's food; which makes me hungry the more I think about it. Miguel's house phone rings and I look at the call id, it's Miguel. I answer it as Nia walks to my side, holding a wet rag in her damp hands.

Miguel speaks calmly but in code, just as I taught him. He tells me that there is someone that is in his office, about to interview for a job, and that she rode in on a silver bike that I should check out. When I confirm in a way befitting a normal confirmation, he continues to say in code that the O.G.'s will be there to bring me to the wash. With that he hangs up the phone and my eyebrows tighten from my brain processing the news.

"Who was it? What's happening?"

"Miguel just talked to me in code. Frankie might be making his move."

My fear that Frankie couldn't wait to send his crew and sends someone else after me might have just been confirmed. This way, Frankie isn't personally crossing the mafia's territory lines and breaking the peace with the other families. Bodies would be showing up in the news full of bullet holes otherwise and I haven't seen or heard anything like that. The good news is that Miguel didn't say anything about Tina's partner, so that rules out that thought. The bad news is that Frankie's crew is full of loyal, big jocks, so whoever this mystery woman is she has to be trouble to be sent in their place. And if she is trouble I hope she's just a punk with a gun, not a professional.

"What's going on?" Nia asks.

"Stay inside." I take Miguel's black Ruger GS32-N handgun for protection and shove it in my pants pocket.

"No. Whatever is, don't go," Nia pleads holding my hand. "I see it in your face, it's something bad."

I slip free from her spongy hold. "I got to go to work. Help will be outside."

"Wait!"

"What," I ask her, my annoyance clear in my tone.

"When the hell are you going to teach me some damn secret codes?"

"Fine, you want a code? Ok, you can use…meet you at the pool house."

"Ok, what does that mean?"

"That means stay inside the damn house!"

"I hate you DeAndre!"

"Yeah, yeah."

"Be careful, asshole!"

I don't look back when I open and close the door behind me, it'd be too hard on me. And I have to be ready, killing someone takes commitment.

The O.G.s arrive in front of Miguel's house a minute later in their green Lowrider. Leaving one guy outside to guard the house, I give him instructions to just hang out on the porch and subtly tell him to stay away from Nia with a joke about her being in a bad mood.

During the drive I keep my hands in my sweats and don't give the hydraulic switches a second look. Not that the fellas were at their peak in regards to attention; their red eyes show me that they smoked a little something before getting a call from Miguel. I keep my mind on the task ahead of me, ignoring the gyro-scented air that has my stomach thinking about what dish Tina is going to prepare.

We pass old Caribbean women selling oranges, pineapples, and mangoes from old shopping carts. A homeless guy in sweaty t-shirts, ripped running pants, and barely-there sneakers, carrying plastic bags with clinking bottles inside, is checking recycling bins. To survive, you do what you have to.

Not five minutes later I'm dropped off a block away from Miguel's carwash; there are a good number of cars waiting in line. The O.G.s drive away, starting to circle the block. As I walk toward the carwash, I see that the cars waiting in line are screened by two greeters at the entrance, so the crowd is controlled. And I assume that the workers will take an extra minute to vacuum the inside of the cars clean, so if anyone is carrying anything they'll know about it. And I see that the hand wash section is the perfect place to isolate unfamiliar faces with the help of Angel and Cinnamon. A carwash is a perfect place for security when done right.

But then my eyes are hit by a glare. I block the glare with my hand and then I see that it's from a silver motorcycle parked in front of Miguel's office.

"Shit." I remember why I am here and run inside.

I stop in front of Miguel's office and I'm happy to see him alive. But the butterflies in my stomach return when I see that he's talking with the biker. She's off somehow. I don't know if it's the yellowish-brown skin and the rough black hair—she's definitely not local to Queens, but Mexico, maybe. From my point of view, her long, black curly hair is shaved on the left side. Some kind of modern punk style, I guess.

I'm curious about the reason why Miguel would keep pretending to interview her personally. Then I watch as Miguel eyes look down at her chest on occasion when she gestures to Angel's picture in the employee of the month plaque on the wall.

It would explain why the biker can be lounging right now, resting her boots on his desk like she is in a living room.

I begin to think that it's a false alarm, but I have to make sure. I knock on the door and then immediately open it; I can't afford to wait for his permission. "Hey."

Miguel replies gesturing to her, "This is the women I was talking about, bro."

The hyena tattoo on the back of the woman's neck has my attention. The design has a true artist's graceful and artful touch despite it being a wild and gruesome animal; I can relate. Then I see that the bare part of her head has a razor thin, fresh scar across it; the few scabs around it date the wound by a few weeks. It's too wide to be from the razor from a haircut gone wrong. Someone took a shot at her and missed. I'm thinking they didn't have an opportunity to take another shot as I look at the definition of her toned arms.

She looks at me with a great smile, working the hot biker chick appeal in her black, low cut v-neck shirt under a leather vest, and tight jeans that would make Tanya jealous. She's in her twenties at least, but she's wearing no cosmetics or perfume from what I can tell. Then I'm drawn to her light brown eyes. Her eyes are cold, as if her soul has been beaten out of her; something I've had much practice recognizing in Africa.

I reach into my pocket and take out the gun. She quickly gets up, standing nearly as tall as me, and kicks the gun out of my hand just as I pull it out. "Damn!" She kicks me hard in the stomach with perfect form. The sting is like nails plunging into my abdomen. I fall to my knees, covering my stomach. "Oh…shit," I mutter.

I block her follow up kick to my face with my arms as Miguel jumps over his desk and hold her from behind to give me time to recover. I'm not one hundred percent ready for this fight but I need to get payback.

I stand up just as she stomps on Miguel's feet, punches him in the groin, and head butts him in the face to break his hold. The different noises he makes would be funny if I was watching it in a comedy show on television.

"Hey, I'm not through with you," I yell. She kicks me hard in the stomach again and I drop to the floor again, emitting my own comedic groan; I wonder if the image of her leather boots is indented on my stomach now.

I see Miguel try to grab for her legs, but she punches him in the head several times. I imagine with the silver rings on her hands her punches are like tiny hammers bruising his thick forehead. I get up and kick her in her side to get her off him and then I push her against the wall. I charge at her and get a few shots in her sides while she only puts her hands up to cover her face and laughs in a horrible, uneven pitch.

I know why she's laughing. Her body is solid muscle and I'm not making a dent. The strain in my arms is building as I continue to punch her, making me slower and slower. She catches me off guard as she suddenly decides to dodge my last punch. She punches my exposed side multiple times before hitting me with an uppercut. As my chin starts to sting, I swing wildly at her, but the punch is unfocused and she makes me pay for it with a knee to the face.

I see a flash and then I hear a buzzing in my ears as I fall to the ground. For a moment, I imagine I'm fighting with my father again as I taste blood in my mouth and there's nothing I can do about it. He was a big man like me, at his prime. I briefly relive his dark, massive hands grabbing me and throwing me around the house; I quickly saw that patrolling in the sun all day didn't help with his skin or his mood.

I snap back to my senses only to see the Hyena jumping toward me with a clenched fist. I roll away in time but the wooden board she hits splits into two pieces. I'm living in five second increments. I'm out of my element.

I crawl away from her as Miguel gets up. She does a spin kick to his face and I watch Miguel slam into the filing cabinet and fall to the floor along with several folders of his reports. The Hyena, for a split second, laughs at Miguel's circumstances and then walks to me purposefully until a gunshot misses her head by a few inches and makes a dent into the wall. Even with my blurry vision, I see a grimace on her face as more voices echo into the room. I then watch as she flings herself out the window facing the lobby; there is something she's afraid of.

Some of the staff runs inside the room, but they are too late. I hear her start the motorcycle and ride it away. She's gone, but I know she'll be back, because I'm still alive.

While Miguel is getting helped up, I slowly wobble to my feet, groaning at every motion I make. "No worries…I got it. No need to help."

Miguel sits on his desk with a heavy thump like an out of shape fireman as he wipes the blood away from his nose. "Who the hell…was that?"

"She's a contract killer." I can't help but think she's more than that. Its one thing to kill with a rifle, but it's another thing to go in and out of places with only your bare hands. But it looks like she's smart enough to know when to leave when the odds are against her. She's definitely a professional.

Miguel and I look at each other and there is an understanding. No more waiting, Nia and I have to leave New York.

MIGUEL AND I hobble inside his house, bandaged and accompanied by Angel and Cinnamon, the only nurses we could afford. Nia is clapping along to new age Christian music playing on her cell phone in the dining room, which has brightened her mood since this morning as she has cleaned up the place a bit; the carpet is vacuumed and the windows are washed.

She hasn't changed out of her short-sleeved gray Mets shirt, black sweats, and white socks with dust building on the bottom. She reminds me of our mother when I would visit when our father was away, but I concentrate on the present pain.

She screams when she turns around and notices us watching her. She turns off the music. "Jesus save me, don't you people ever knock?"

"What do you mean, you people?" I joke. She's not amused but I don't care; it was funny.

"Wait...what the hell happen to you? And who are these whores?"

I stand in front Angel and Cinnamon and stop the potential catfight that is bound to happen. "We got into a fight and they're friends. Let's keep the peace, ok, everyone?" I stagger towards Nia as the ladies walk Miguel to the living room.

"Why are you walking funny?" Nia asks.

I laugh, but only for a moment. It hurts my chest too much. "A well-trained fighter did this."

"A guy just strolled into the place and did that?" She points to my bruises in disbelief.

"A woman, if you want to be specific."

"A woman kicked your ass? Damn." She walks to me and helps me walk by holding my arm.

"Sexist. And she was built like a gladiator." We make our way to the nearest chair and I sit down.

"I'm just saying…what happen to all that traditional training?"

"There's a difference between strategic training and tactical training, Nia."

"Is this where you sound smart about something, DeAndre?"

She can always make me smile. I think I always like how her brutal honesty clashes with my bullshit. "Yes, actually."

"Cliff notes, please."

"That's real easy. Strategy is about making the plans and…" I moan from the pain from my stomach.

"Which one gets you less visits to the hospital?"

I sigh and reply, "We can't go to the hospital right now."

"Are you stupid?"

I sigh again, rubbing my hands against each other. "We have to leave, it's getting too dangerous."

"No shit, but you are still hurt," Nia comments.

"We have no bullet holes and we can take a couple of hits from a woman, ok?"

"Sexist," Nia replies; I look at her and she smiles. I scoff at her. "Ok then, explain your company."

"Miguel needs to talk to Angel, the one with the blonde hair." I smile as Nia scuffs at the name, ready to rant on the irony I imagine.

"Why?"

"She's pregnant." I'm still amazed that Miguel took the news well in the mist of Angel's panic attack after seeing him bruised, forcing her to open up about her secret and need for financial support if he wants the baby. He had no doubt in his mind about the truth of the news. They apparently had too much of a good time in the Champagne Room.

"Of course she is pregnant. Are they going to keep the baby?"

"They're talking about it."

"Oh, I'm getting involved in this talk."

I grab her arm and stop her from causing more drama. "You're doing nothing but leaving them alone to have…"

"Have what, an abortion? He needs to stand right by that baby!"

"Leave it alone." She struggles against my hold.

"Let go of me!" She yells, still unable to break free.

I'm having a sense of déjà vu from this morning looking into her eyes of defiance. "This isn't one your elementary classrooms. These are adults, so leave them alone."

"Fine. You can get tell me later about what happen to those targets' children after you get down from your high horse."

I've told her too much, but the boredom and her constant nagging to open up can be hell for even a sniper's patience. I let her go; I've already endured enough abuse today. Besides, I always try dancing around the topic of babies with her. I know the subject is like a dagger to her heart because she can't have any.

I see her walk to toward the living room, ready to testify with righteousness. But she stops as Angel and Cinnamon storm past her, open, and close the door. Miguel walks out of the living room and has a conversation with Nia. The questions in my head are answered as Nia screams with excitement and hugs him, almost making him fall over from the embrace.

She dances with him in celebration and it's hilarious. It's like watching a trainer making a large dog stand on its hind legs for the first time. But Miguel still carries on, embarrassing himself, as Nia laughs pleasantly. They stop as the door is knocked upon heavily. Nia runs and hides behind me as I stand up.

Miguel sneaks a peek at the window and then gives me a reassuring look.

"Who is it?" Nia whispers.

"Just stay behind me," I answer her.

"And what are you going to do?" She asks me.

"Look tough." I tighten my lips, narrow my eyes, and raise my left eyebrow.

She leans forward and looks at me. "What the hell is that?"

"Are you kidding me right now?"

"You look stupid," Nia replies.

Miguel looks at us in amazement as the door is knocked on again.

"I got this, Nia. Miguel, open the door brother."

"Miguel, don't open the door. Stop with the look."

"I got this, alright?"

"Jesus, save me," she relies.

"Alright," I ask again firmly.

She stands up straight. "Oh yeah, you got this, you're the man."

"Miguel, open the door." I give the look as Nia sighs.

Miguel opens the door, showing that Lungile is standing in front of three black men.

Fresh from the airport, all of them are wearing brown suits and one of them is carrying suitcases. I see that the teenager I left is now little man. Lungile's hair is cut low and evenly. He has more weight in his face and muscles on his body. Lungile looks at me with a grin, but I'm distracted by his face being marked by a two-inch scar, like one a rebel's machete would leave behind.

As my face relaxes, my mind begins to build appropriate questions to ask him but stops when Tina and Maria walk behind them with a pot of food in their hands. Their timing is perfect because I'm lost for words at Lungile's transformation. To my surprise, Lungile orders the two men with nothing in their hands to help them and they follow his instruction.

Following his lead, I order, "Nia, show our guests to the kitchen."

Nia hits the side of my head before she walks into the kitchen; only my pride is hurt. Maria and the two men walk inside and follow Nia. As Lungile and Miguel shake hands, making their introductions, Tina walks to me quickly.

She asks, "What happened to you?" I'm taken aback by her careful inspection of my wounds and wraps.

"I didn't know you cared."

"I'm a nurse, smart guy…remind me to come back later and get some better bandages for you."

She's a nurse? It explains the default kindness yesterday. I'll check her background later to make sure. "Any chance you can add painkillers to that order?"

Chapter 9: Picking Up An Old Friend

THE GOOD side of leaving early on a Monday morning is that only people with jobs and children are up. Plus, the line in the coffee shop is short. I get my usual medium hot chocolate with four sugars and creams; it's not like I am expecting vitamins and nutrients in a place selling glazed snacks by the dozen.

I'm happy that I'm not driving as the milk chocolate goodness goes down my throat. Lungile is beside me eating a chocolate doughnut in the backseat of their leased, black, four-door Audi R8. His bodyguard in the passenger seat plays with the car radio, going back and forth between stations, and I'm getting anxious to pick up Black Widow sooner. I take another sip to relax my nerves.

The bad side is that we're going to Harlem, which is a little too close to Melrose for my liking, but it's the one place I can send Black Widow. When I started in this business, all I needed was to obtain an import permit from the ATF, pay for the paperwork, and have patience. But now, Black Widow needs to be taken apart and mailed to my gym trainer; Black Widow would be linked to too many deaths otherwise. The good news is that my friends at the gym aren't Frankie's friends, so Black Widow is in good hands.

Lungile asks, "So tell me again about this man who beat you up."

"It was a woman," I correct him.

His men laugh until he slaps then both in the back of the head; respect for me, I hope. They are ten years older than him, maybe in their late twenties from the early signs of balding, but they shut up quickly. His guards aren't that much to look at, barely bigger than Nia. But to get slapped into silence that easily means that Lungile has moved up in ranks from last I saw him.

"Can you describe her to me?" Lungile asks.

"My resources say that she's Peruvian. Aggression and fighting is tradition where she comes from, as is her squeaky laugh."

What I don't tell him is that because of limited funds, my resource is YouTube. It was only through luck that I found the video from VICE, "Fist Fighting on Christmas: A Peruvian Tradition." All the pieces came together when I saw that video: the attraction to leather because of her people's horse riding history, the laughing is to mask her identity, and her fighting style is from their Takanakuy celebration which allows kicks and punches. Apparently, she needs more than one day of fighting to get a rush out of life.

"How else will I recognize her?" Lungile asks.

"Other than the one side of her head being shaved because of a bullet scar, she'll be the one kicking my ass in leather pants if we ever meet again in an unarmed fight." I would normally go into a joke, but the way he looks at me coldly, taking long slow sips of his black coffee, tells me to do otherwise. His calm demeanor is like a man that has seen death so many times that it becomes easy to talk about it like sports; he's one of us, a killer.

He replies simply, "I'll take care of her for you."

"You've been practicing."

"Of course," he says, finally smiling.

We take a look outside as we park in front of the gym, the one place where people would go this early in this area to do something physically productive and legal. I unbuckle my seatbelt.

"I'll be back in a flash…"

"Stay. My men will take care of it." He takes a sip of coffee.

"It's all good, my man inside…" Lungile looks at me, as do his guards. I know the argument is over.

"What is his name?" Lungile asks.

"Dan. He'll be short, but have a lot of upper body muscle, glasses…"

Lungile speaks to his men in their native tongue and his men leave my car in a hurry. I'm rusty, but I think the basic tone was that they aren't to make him wait. We both watch his men enter the gym and I briefly hear, through the open window, the banging of weights hitting racks and rock music. I can only hope Dan doesn't start any trouble or at least goes to the window to confirm that I'm with them.

"Do you think I can get her?"

"What?"

Lungile motions towards the gym and I scan inside. I see among the muscle heads a young girl walking back and forth, getting pumped before doing a squat; three hundred pounds by my guess. She looks like a normal girl in her ponytails, but her muscle mass makes it hard to tell her age; she could be a teenager maintaining her femininity around her muscle.

We watch her do her set from beginning to end and he says, "She is like a rock hammer."

"Yeah...I guess."

After her set she gets high fives as she laughs and sticks her tongue out at people. I look at Lungile as he continues to gaze at her and my stomach turns. I recall Abasi saying similar words before a random woman got picked from the street and was never seen again.

"I will have her." My concerns about his intentions are fully answered when I see him lick his lips and grin.

"Listen, Lungile..." I pause as Lungile unbuckles his seatbelt. "American girls are..."

He turns to me and smiles briefly, but then he yells, "DeAndre!"

He lunges towards me, moves my head away, and pushes a silver Colt M1911 pistol with a silencer toward the passenger headrest when a shot is taken. I now realize that someone is behind me and Lungile is struggling for control of the gun. I hear the gun rattle on the ground. Lungile groans from the struggle, getting punches to the face I assume. I get my confirmation when Lungile is thrown back to his seat with a swelling eye and cut lip.

I see two white forearms quickly move past my head, wrap a wire around my neck, and tighten it. I fight against his hold and dig into the wire with my fingers, blocking the pain as it scrapes against my skin.

I kick against my seat and push myself through the window and onto the ground. I see the gun by his feet and the temptation to reach for it and shoot this guy in the head is incalculable. But feeling the thickness of the metal rubbing against my throat I instead decide to try to break my attempted murderer's hold by elbowing him in the chest. Since he has to lower himself to keep the hold, I'm going to make him pay for it. As I start to gag from the process, my priority changes back to making my hands burn to keep the wire away from my neck. I look up to see my attacker and all I can see is a white chin and a gray hood.

"Let him go," Lungile yells before he exits the car on his side.

The tension around the wire loosens and I can move my neck. I see my attacker backing off as I take deep breaths and remove the wire. I see my attacker and Lungile are in a standoff, their guns pointed at each other. I can't believe that my attacker is lucky enough to have picked up the gun in time to prevent Lungile getting the drop on him with his midnight black 9 mm pistol. I look closer at the attacker's right hand tattoo, a reaper. He's a Goddamn government ghost or, more likely, he used to be, just like my former trainer.

"Who are you, tell me," Lungile orders.

"He's a hit man and the price on my head has to be at least fifty thousand by now," I answer for the Ghost. It looks like Frankie is doing his homework for his puppets, considering this close call.

Anyone could be after me right now: couples with kids, struggling artists, or drug addicts, all of them needing to make their lives better. I touch my throat, I'm not sure if the blood is from my hand or neck.

The Ghost slowly walks backwards as people start to panic and scream, hiding in their cars as they stop traffic. But as Lungile's men run out of the gym, he shoots Lungile's gun out his hand and turns his gun toward me, but Lungile's men prevent him from taking a shot by shooting at him with their 9 mm pistols. They miss but they make him run away with an athlete's speed, to my amazement.

Lungile picks up his gun and starts to aim, but the Ghost runs across the street and disappears into the crowd of panicked people in a matter of moments.

"Damn it!" Lungile yells with frustration.

I look at Lungile as he looks at his hand more than at me. "I'm fine, by the way."

"Sorry about that, bruder." He helps me up and into the car just as his men run into car, but then he yells to the crowd, "Remember my face, because I'll remember yours! If I see my face in the news, your family will see yours in the grave!" He gets in the car and slams the door. "Drive!"

As we peel away into traffic, Lungile yells orders in their native tongue to the driver. As they break every law of the road, they look for the Ghost. I look outside and it's not going to be an easy task, he wore a gray running suit but so is every other person jogging the streets; the Ghost's reason for wearing the running suit in the first place I assume. Lungile continues to yell orders. The basic translation I get is simple enough for anyone to follow: Find him, catch him, and kill him.

Chapter 10: The Last Meal

AFTER HOURS of bleeding on my clothes and not finding anyone close to the Ghost's description, Lungile's men give my throat and hands the bandages they've been aching and oozing for; war makes every soldier know basic first aid. With Lungile's apologies and his assurances that they would be ready in a moment's notice, they drop me off in front of Miguel's place.

I walk toward the front door and smell chicken and tomato coming from the open window; watching only a few cooking shows over the weekend and Miguel suddenly takes after his mother in the kitchen, thank God for that. I knock on the door, barely able to make a fist.

Nia gasps after she answers the door, "What the hell is this?" She reaches out to touch the bandages on my throat. "What happened to you?"

"Shish."

The television is on and is covering the story. The reporter is interviewing angry residents yelling about gun violence and the city's problems with poverty and gangs. The reporter says that the investigators working on the case have no working image of what the suspects look like, but encourage citizens to go to the police department if they would like to become witnesses for the case. It's not going to happen and they know it.

Nia touches my throat and I groan from the pain. I move her hand away, only to endure prickly pain from my fingers when my hand presses against her hand. "How was your day," I ask her as I walk in, the smell of the tomato sauce is richer and more distinct.

After I hear her close the door behind me, she replies, "You come in here looking like shit, again, and you want to know how my day was?"

She takes my arm, puts it over her small shoulders, and slowly walks me towards a chair by the living room table. I turn off the television as the news starts to cover a flash mob in Time Square dancing in their t-shirts and underwear for a new clothing product. I like that plates, utensils, three open bottles of water, and paper napkins are already laid out. I'm starving, enough to eat lunch and dinner.

Miguel walks out of the kitchen with a breadbasket and a bowl of Fideua. He takes one look at me and shakes his head side to side. He puts the bowls on the table and sits down.

"I'm fine by the…ow…"

"Sorry," Nia says as she adjusts her hold away from my still aching side.

She sits me down and sits next to me. "Seriously, you look like shit."

"Too hungry to talk, I want some Fideua."

I smile even though she looks at me with narrowing eyes. "Serve it yourself."

She holds my hand and Miguel's hand. Miguel then holds my other hand. "What's happening…why am I being tortured?" Miguel presses my hand tightly for a second. "Hey, man!"

"Stop it the two of you! Show some respect," Nia comments.

We're older than her and yet we are the ones bowing our heads down first; old habits, like listening to woman with authority, die hard. Nia says a nice prayer, her voice respectful and her tone thoughtful. Afterwards, my hands know mercy when they let go of them. Miguel quickly serves himself a plate.

I look at my hands and sigh at the thought of holding a fork. "I'll just order come fried chicken cutlets or something." I reach for Miguel's landline phone at the end of the table, but Miguel swats my hand with a fork. "Ok…really?"

"No calls, remember? We might get traced," Nia taunts before she helps herself to the Fideua, removing the mushrooms from the angel hair pasta before putting it on her plate. She enjoys herself as she takes her first fork full, moaning loudly with pleasure, and I roll my eyes. With food in her mouth, she says, "The tomato sauce and parsley make everything taste so…fantastic."

As my stomach grumbles, I mutter, "I hate you both."

Indifferent, she takes a bite of a red pepper slice. "Miguel, is that garlic I taste?"

I reply, "If I could get a forkful into my mouth, I can confirm for you."

She looks at me briefly, before turning her attention back to Miguel. "So, Miguel, is every ok with…what's the woman's name again?"

I bang the table to get her attention with my hands. "Ow!"

Mumbling curses is the only thing I can do as my hands pulse and the bandages start to have a thin red discharge on them from clenching my fists. But I hope they understand my needs now, no matter how childish. Nia slowly looks at me as Miguel sits quietly, cleaning up the water that is still spilling out from my water bottle with a paper napkin until he stands the bottle up.

She sighs as she wraps a large amount of pasta around her fork. "Say ah."

"I'm not a child."

"No, you're a big boy," she says in a baby voice.

She smiles when I give in, open my mouth, and eat what's on the fork. She uses her free hand to wipe my mouth clean with a napkin. "A parent's job is to steer their children into cleanliness."

In response I chew with my mouth open. I relish in her sneer. Miguel once asked me why Nia and I were so different. I wonder if my explanation makes sense now. Our parents were more involved with her after they were saved by Christianity, so she grew up as a child who believed in the best in people and became judgmental to those stuck in their ways of sin. But during my childhood, our parents were absent, abusive, and sad people. My childhood was, at best, unhappy. Then again, to have my sister grow up not being able to have children, while I choose not to have any because of my upbringing, still proves to me that God is a comedian.

Miguel takes a largest piece of bread and slowly feeds it to me. After I am able to get it in my mouth, I mutter a barely audible, "Thank you."

We all share a laugh. The moment is silly, but some of the best things in life are best left unsaid. Nia's cell phone rings and stops the laughter. Her ringtone is a religious song I wish I could remember so that I could mock it.

"Don't tell them where you are," I quickly comment.

"Yeah, I got it. Just don't kick my legs like at Tina's place."

I still watch her answer the phone to make sure she doesn't make a mistake.

"Hello. Hello?"

I tense up as she looks at me as her eyebrows lower, she looks at a complete loss about something. "Who is it? They just hung up," I ask her. She looks at her phone and nods with confirmation.

I wipe my mouth with a napkin, ignoring the pain, before I get up and walk to the corner of the window near the front door. I scan pass all the cars parked in the street and zoom toward the two rows of four silver motor cycles that are in front of the house, the riders are wearing helmets and they are all looking towards me.

"Miguel!"

The lead driver drives away and the rest follow, zooming by with a thunderous boom from the joint sounds of their engines.

"Are we in trouble?" Nia asks.

I turn around and Miguel is already in his liquor cabinet, taking out a small bottle of painkillers from Tina, his old black and brown AK-47 machine gun, and the black Ruger GS32-N handgun.

"You have a machine gun? That's been there the whole time?" Nia yells.

Miguel hands me the bottle first, then the handgun.

Nia gets up and walks toward us as we check for ammo. "Let's just get out of here!"

It was the Hyena, it had to be. She'll never stop until I'm dead. All professionals see a contract through. I tell Nia calmly, "Nia, start packing our stuff and smash your phone."

"You're lucky I back up my numbers on-line," Nia comments.

I watch as she throws her phone to the floor and smashes it into pieces. "You could have just put it on the table, used a hammer, and threw it in the trash. But that's fine too," I mention.

"Wait, are my friends safe?" Nia asks.

"Yes," I answer I put my attention back to looking outside.

"How do you know?" Nia asks.

"You would have been sent pictures of them with a gun to their heads," I answer bluntly.

The impact of my words doesn't fully register with me until I look at Miguel and he gives me a brief look of disappointment. I look back at Nia as her mouth is open from shock.

"Forget what I said."

Nia turns her back to me and runs down into the basement. I look down at the floor.

TWENTY minutes later, no signs of any motor bikes. The O.G.'s are driving around the block now, sending a message that we are ready. But nothing happens. I clean up Nia's mess and I go downstairs. I see that Nia is putting the last of the bags together.

"Are you all done?" I ask.

"Oh, you mean putting your own shit together? Yup," Nia snaps back at me, zipping my luggage bag only halfway through until it gets stuck.

I place the gun between my back and belt, walk to her, and press the top of the bag down with my hands. She doesn't look at me as she zips the bag completely sealed. "Are you ok?"

"Just peachy and you," Nia answers as she piles her bags together; just making herself busy from the looks of it.

"If you want to get your frustration out on me you can," I suggest with little expectation that she would follow through.

But she faces me, punches me in the stomach and slaps me in the face. And because I am already hurt I actually have to cover myself from her tiny hands. "Ok, Nia." She's not listening to me, because she's too busy cursing at me. "Ok, Nia! Ok, Nia!" I hold her hands and see her eyes water. "I get it. Do you feel better now?"

She stomps my right foot and I fall unto the mattress like freshly cut timber. "Now I feel better!" As I rub my foot she stands over me like a conqueror with her hands on her hips. "And you're buying me a new phone when this is done!" She kicks my other foot, for good measure or just because she can. Then she walks pass me and stomps upstairs. I turn my head to make sure she's gone and I see Miguel is sitting on the stairs watching me.

"Where were you?" I yell at Miguel.

"I was here, watching you get your ass kicked by your little sister," Miguel comments bluntly, but I see him fighting a smile.

Chapter 11: The Diner

MY CAR DIDN'T earn me much credit in the chop shop, so Miguel's gives his truck without a second thought. There are no special instructions except that it needs gas soon. I leave a message with Lungile to meet us when I find a lodge or hotel in Pennsylvania near the woods, somewhere nice and close to God's country and away from prying eyes.

After briefly watching Nia say her preachy goodbye to Miguel, stating that she's going to leave the rosary at his door for protection, I start placing the bags in the back of the truck. I then carefully hide Black Widow in the back seat, and topping it with a plastic bag of medicine bottles with a mix of pills inside, a last favor from Tina.

I stop Nia from her rant by slapping hands with Miguel and share a bro hug with a double back tap combo. "Be good, man," I comment.

"Be safe, brother."

"Can a sister get a hug," Nia asks with a smile.

I guess Nia is demoralized when it come to the three of us. Nia always has been the small one around me, that's why I'm use to her yelling to get attention. I watch as she gets a bear hug from Miguel. As he briefly plucks her up and makes her squeal before being put down, I smile; be careful what you ask for.

Nia and I get into the truck and drive away, getting an escort for a few blocks with the O.G.s before going our separate ways.

Then our stomachs a noise, we briefly look at each other. From the rush, we forgot to eat and bring food. Despite my gut, I still park Miguel's truck in front of the Over the Bridge Diner when it appears up the road. Besides, of all the stupid, irresponsible things we could have done, fainting while driving would have been on the top five. It is a small place between Rockefeller Center in Midtown and Central Park, past the Ed Koch Queensboro Bridge.

We go inside and I smell fish and French fries cooking in oil, Miguel would love this place. There are mostly old guys inside sitting down, talking to each other at leisure, the advantage of retirement.

Nia walks pass me. "Where are you going," I ask her.

"Ah, the bathroom maybe...hello, duh," Nia replies back.

After watching her turn the corner, I take the table that the waitress points to. "Two waters please." She places two menus on top of the table and walks away with a pleasant smile, I smile back until she turns her back at me; the syrup stains on the menus just cost her a good tip.

I notice that the people around me either have scar tissue on their faces, a handicap, or on their bare arms from wearing short sleeve, yellow and black, Hawaiian shirts are Army and Navy tattoos. But they aren't made men; their solemn faces while drinking their coffee tell a different story.

After ten minutes pass, I'm weary of seeing the waitress hovering around the table waiting for me to signal her to take my order. After looking at the menu for the tenth time, something about Nia being gone this long bothers me. I get up, walk to the other side of the Diner, and I see Nia dancing with an old man with a bent back and a prosthetic foot. The song they are dancing to on a jukebox is a fast beat song from the eighties, but it doesn't matter; the old man not only looks like a turtle but moves like one too. But I see Nia giving him enough of an encouraging smile to get him moving.

I make sure I'm invisible to her as I stay close to the wall. I'm pretty sure she doesn't know I'm watching because her smile hasn't left. In watching her in her innocence I remember why I'm defensive of her; she's the only one left in our family. And despite my qualities she still loves me. With the exception of Miguel, of all of the people that have christen me as brother she's the one that means it the most because I don't have to make her laugh, amuse her, or owe her a favor for her to love me. Although she's the one person I love to make laugh, because she makes me work for it the most.

As I let her have her fun with her dance partner, I remember when she was a little kid at home slightly swaying back and forth to rap music for the first time, it made everyone laugh.

When the music stops, she gives her dance partner a hug and I see the man smile a toothless smile. As the old man leaves, a Bobby Brown song plays. Before I can name the title, I see a young man stand up from a booth in a black turtleneck, khaki pants, and leather shoes. He approaches her and makes her smile as he starts dancing.

"Oh, here we go," I comment, seeing anything playboy in action.

I can't see his face, but I can see his intention through his hips and in Nia's grin as she dances with him. I walk toward them and I can't wait to put the scare of God into him. Our mother use to identify actions like this as male stupidity, but taking opportunities to play big brother has its fun moments.

The guy looks young, college or out a few years. He's white, clean shaven, and smooth on top, but looks like a cartoon villain because of his black turtleneck shirt. I'm taken aback that he dances well, not mechanically at all. He actually has rhythm. So, when he touches her hip, I know it's not for coordination. As I continue watch his hand, I notice it has a reaper tattoo. He's the Ghost. I see red and his small neck is my target.

I slowly creep behind him, my eyes narrowing. My hands are aching for payback.

"Oh, hey, bro," Nia says apologetically.

The Ghost turns around and sees me behind him; his smile goes away. Nia screams as I grab his neck and squeeze. Before I can lift him up and raise him to my eye level to watch him suffer, he breaks my hold with well-aimed hits against my wrists and pushes me away. We look at each and get into fighting positions, raising our hands on guard.

I'm dying to kick someone's ass right now, just to remind myself that I can still do it. But I'm patient, waiting for him to make the first move and mistake; unfortunately so is he. Nia steps in front of me and slaps me in the face, like I stole something from her.

"Get out of the way, Nia," I yell at her.

"He was just dancing with me!"

I move her aside by the arm and the Ghost is gone. "What the hell?" I look at the booth he was sitting at and he left cash on the table.

"The first decent guy I've seen all day…"

"Who the hell…" I begin to yell and then look around at the growing concern of the veterans. I fake a smile and yell, "Sorry, folks, my sister."

I pay the waitress for her trouble as she approaches us before I grab Nia by the hand and drag her outside, still keeping calm as the veterans are sure to still be watching us.

"I know you're pissed, but I needed to…"

"That was him."

"Who is he?"

I stop dragging her before I open the passenger seat and point to my neck. "That gave me this, Nia. This!"

"I didn't know…how was I supposed know? You don't tell me anything!"

"Get in the truck!" I look down to calm myself; the alternative is to throw her inside the truck. Thankfully, she gets in without argument and I slam the door.

"Don't slam the door at me!" I sigh as I'm blessed with the windows being up and her voice being partly muffled, making me stand in place instead of walking around the truck and getting inside. Nia yells, adding, "And we still didn't eat!"

My stomach heard that clearly as it growls loudly. "Shit."

"Did you hear me?"

"We'll go through a drive through!" I mentally punish myself for not thinking of that in the first place.

"I don't want to eat any burgers!"

"Then eat chicken!"
"Then get in the truck!"
"Then...you...fine!"

Chapter 12: Checking In

"ARE YOU FOLKS here for the fourth of July celebrations?" the front desk clerk asks me.

I can't believe I forgot that it's a holiday, but frankly I'm still adjusting from being stuck with Nia on the road to really care. "That and to get some Sunbury's souvenirs," I reply with a smile.

We share a pleasant laugh as Nia finishes signing in as Ms. Smith. After a few more minutes of pleasant chatting about the dead deer head set up behind the clerk, the hotel's bellgirl arrives and I take pleasure in seeing her walk. She starts to load the cart with our bags, but when I help her with the task she gives me a slight smile; the kind that makes me hopeful of my chances of a hook up.

Nia and I are then led to our first floor rooms as the bellgirl carts our bags behind her. I look the bellgirl up and down at her pear shape body. She makes the hotel's brown vest and black pants uniform look better than the clerk did. The bellgirl says a few things about Willow Creek hotel's history, but my only take away is that her feminine voice is lovely to listen to.

Nia elbows me at my side, to remind me why we're here in the first place I'm guessing. But I don't need a reminder. Before deciding to come here, it took twenty minutes for me to convince Nia that her first choice of hotels wasn't ideal; a lodge with a built in water slide inside and people taking pictures at a lavish weddings on the golf course; it just didn't scream low key to me.

This hotel is simple. Per the description from my on-line search using my cell phone, it has two floors, a small court yard with two stone benches for lounging outside, and a small sitting area inside to eat breakfast, lunch, and dinner. The woods are only a few feet away and the town is a mile away to supply food and goods that the hotel can't provide.

Plus, now that I think about it, every cop in this area will be too busy looking for mostly drunk drivers in cars. It would explain why we didn't get any police spot checks at the portions toll before I-80 W or while we were driving around looking for hotels.

Now happier with our situation, we're shown to our rooms, right across from each other, as per my request. The bellgirl reaches for the bags but I take it instead, it only takes a moment for me to take our bags off the cart and next to our beds. Besides, I'm anxious about the one bag that is carrying Miguel's handgun; Black Widow is staying in the truck, for now.

After dropping off the last bag in Nia's room, I give the bellgirl two twenties with a wink and a smile. Before I can ask her when it's a good time for her to come back to my room, Nia snatches a twenty and puts it in her pants pocket with no apparent shame.

"Do the actual work next time and then you can get the full tip!" Then Nia closes the door on the bellgirl's face, ruining any chance I might have with the bellgirl.

"Why would you do that?" I don't know why I bother asking Nia questions like that.

Nia turns to me and replies, "I wanted the lodge with the slide and you wanted to hook up with her. It looks like no one is going to be happy tonight." She snaps her fingers at me and walks to her bed.

"Listen, Nia, it's my life, so if I want to…"

"If you want a distraction from your life, read a bible."

I watch as Nia go through her carry on bag and take out a picture from her purse. She puts the picture up against the corner of the window above the dresser and then she tests her bed's coils by bouncing on it at different spots. Taking a closer look at the picture I see it's from our only family trip at Disney World.

"In a different universe, you would still be dressing up as a princess," I comment before looking back at Nia.

"And you would still be dressing up as a pirate. Looks like we're stuck with the versions we are now. How much time did the clerk say he'll leave the kitchen open for us," Nia asks, sitting still in the center of the bed, looking at me.

"We have been in a truck for over five hours. Don't you want to sleep, settle in, or…sleep?" My mind and my body is still slightly recovering from the pot holes and traffic during the drive.

"Sleep with only junk food in my stomach? I don't think so."

"Oh my God," I mutter with my hands rubbing my aching eyes.

Before I know it I'm getting hit by a pillow. I uncover my eyes and see Nia is standing in front of me, about to take a swing at me again with a pillow in her hand. I grab the pillow, pull it out of her hands, and hit her sides several times with the pillow. She runs to the bed and rolls up into a ball, laughing. The more she laughs the more I hit her with the pillow; although it does make me smile. I finally surrender when it becomes a work out and I throw the pillow aside.

"Well?" She asks looking back at me.

I sigh. "Thirty more minutes."

"Then we only have ten minutes to clean up."

I roll my eyes, turn around, and walk away. I'm not going to argue, I'm not hungry but I can eat something small and light for public impressions. She surprises me with a hug from behind after she jumps on my back. I just stand still, I'm afraid she'll fall the wrong way if I shake her off. "Ok Nia. It's going to be ok."

"I love that picture, we were all happy that day," she comments.

I look at the picture across from us and then look at our silly image in the mirror. "I remember."

"It's just you and me now, you know," she whispers in my ear, hugging me tighter.

"I know," I reply, holding her hands.

THE NEXT morning, Lungile's last call to me is to tell me that he's close to arriving to the hotel. I've been watching my bedroom windows since then. People have been going in and out of town with bags of fireworks on top of whatever groceries they bought. I leave Nia in her room to indulge in her own wishes with the cable television, so long as she calls my room's phone every hour.

In my boredom, I put ointment on my hands after taking a shower. The scabs over my wounds are cleaning up nicely and the pills from Tina help with the pain. But sitting by myself, I can't help but think about Nia's hug yesterday and her comment about it just being the two of us. She always was family first, a blessing from her upbringing.

Nia didn't steal candy from stores, steal bikes right off the racks, or work as a caddy for months to find the right opportunity to ride the carts off the golf courses. She had her moments, but fun is for the daring and I always wanted more of it. And why shouldn't I? Kids were running numbers in pool shops and barber shops. It was the Clinton years and I didn't care about the law, because my father was there to cover up for me. It always led to a beating at night, but not jail.

Then making deals with gangs became a requirement; they had more guns than I did. That was just the reality of the streets. So, I had to learn to be fast on my feet and work their sets. The more I handled myself and made money, the more people with which I got myself involved. I couldn't stop, I got addicted to it.

Anyone working for the LCF got addicted to it. It was easy, considering we all had troubling relationships with our fathers and no real work history. Except for Miguel and me, very few of us were high school educated. We were young men with nothing to do except earn respect, power, and money in a neighborhood that provides it by very few methods, none of them positive. We didn't have what it took to become strippers—well I did, for a day, but I stopped when everyone called me the playboy, and it stuck.

But no matter what I did, Miguel had my back and still does. What I've always respected about him is that he isn't just a giant with muscles; he has a mind. So, I wasn't surprised when he took over the carwash. He's able to keep people honest and alive, like he did for me growing up. And that's why I went to him when I was looking for a safe place. I trust Miguel with my life with this bounty on my head. He's an incredible friend, he's going to make a good father, and I'm going to spoil his kid rotten.

I lift my head, realizing I'm lost in thought. I causally touch the revolver at my side when someone knocks on my door. "Who is it?"

"It sure ain't Ms. Thing looking for another tip! Now open the damn the door before I eat all this food!"

I get up, walk to the door, peep through the door's hole, and confirm it's just Nia. I slip the gun between my back and my belt. Then I unlock and open the door. "You were supposed to let me know when you want to get something to eat and then we go together. That was the agreement."

She walks in with a plastic tray carrying two dishes of scrambled eggs and bacon, with two small bottles of orange juice, plastic utensils, and a handful of napkins on the side. "Don't make me throw this food on the floor."

I close and lock the door. "Just put it on the bed, please."

"Um hmm," she comments as she places the tray on my bed, sitting down next to it soon after. She takes and eats a piece of bacon. "So, what's up? Talk to me."

I sit down, even though I'm afraid this invitation is really a trap to share more emotions. "Lungile will be here soon, unless he's delayed."

"Delayed doing what?" She asks, raising her left eyebrow.

I blame myself for saying too much. "If they feel that they are being followed, then they'll drive around and hide in nearby neighborhoods, or do whatever until they feel safe."

"Do whatever," she quickly asks. I just pick up a plate, a plastic fork, and I start eating. Maybe if I eat something, maybe she'll do the same and stop talking. She takes a bottle of orange juice, opens it, and takes a sip. "So, we could leave in a few hours then?"

"No. When they get here, we're going to put our heads together and talk…"

Nia laughs in defeat, throwing her hands up briefly in the air, as if calling to God for strength. "What? Were you expecting that we were going to discuss our problems away?"

"Is this where I say the Mafia owns the cops? Is it too soon…no?"

"The big, bad hitman telling me how the world works. Our parents didn't mess you up that much."

"Stop talking about them," I yell, clenching my fists, snapping the fork in the process. She does a double take. "I didn't mean to…"

"Our parents, the only parents this damn world will ever give us, just died. How are we not talking about them? How can you even function?"

"There are different ways to survive." I throw the pieces of the fork to the floor and look over my hand, nothing more than a scratch.

"Like Tanya?"

If she keeps diving into my head any deeper she'll give me a migraine. "Would it be too much to ask just to get some food in my stomach?"

"Did you know that a counselor got dad out of drinking?"

"I'm so glad…"

"He stopped blaming himself for you leaving…"

"Sure, why not."

"And you need to stop blaming him, your pride made you leave the house."

"Daily black eyes made me leave."

"I wondered about that…then I realized something."

"What's that?"

"Sometimes you fight someone because you can see what they're capable of and you try to stop it."

"With his fists?"

"I don't remember him starting with them. Just you were coming home late…"

My checkered past haunts me. "Yeah, yeah…you could have left with me if you were so concerned."

"I was just a kid…"

"So was I." I reply, taken back that I had a little venom in my tone.

After a brief pause, Nia says, "All those times you were sneaking back home…he was across the street in a different car, like in a stake out. He just wanted to take a glimpse at his son while he was growing up." She reaches for my head and I move it away, more from shame than shock. I thought I was being slick sneaking in and out the house, it looks like I was just being blind to the game that was being played.

"I assume everything I told our mother and you in confidence was shared with him."

She moves my head to the side with a light dismissive push; I'll take that as a yes. "There goes the Johnson stubbornness. You're more like daddy than you like to admit."

There's a loud knock on the door. I put the plate on the tray. "Quiet," I whisper.

As I get up and reach for my gun, I hear, "Open up bruder."

Lungile's voice brings comfort to me. I have my back up again and can move on with my plans. I take a look back at Nia with a smile, but she looks down with a frown. Until people start lighting up a few of their fireworks outside, then I watch as Nia looks outside with a smile. A memory of us as children pops up in my head. We were walking to a nearby car garage with her bike's flat tire in my hand and fifty cents in my pocket to have the tire put back into working order and put some air in it. I remember her singing happily when we did.

There's another knock on the door. Nia turns to me and nods her head with approval.

"I'm coming." I finally comment.

Chapter 13: Show Down

JULY FIFTH and I wake up to the sounds of firecrackers and young people laughing outside my window. My dream about lying next to my mother as a child in her bed is quickly fading. The image of her light brown skin radiating from her big cheeks as I poke at them fades. The next image that fades is the image of me tugging at her brown curly hair and her tickling my sides. Her wide smile is the last thing to fade.

As I sit up, I see children jump around. I'm about to yell out the window like the old man my tender bones are confirming that I am; arguing with Lungile about the game plan until one in the morning is not worth the grogginess I feel. I glance at the clock by my bed and it's ten o'clock. I yawn and let the children have their fun. Getting out of bed, I shuffle to the bathroom to brush my teeth and take a shower. I scratch my backside before closing the door behind me.

After doing my bathroom routine, I change into my blue cotton shirt, black pants, and leather shoes; better to keep entertaining the town people's notions that I'm a business man instead of something else.

I give Lungile a call to come down and to drive with me into town to give Frankie a follow up call. As I recall the conversation with Frankie yesterday with Lungile, we wonder why it didn't go well even after sharing the plan of that would provide him more money for the guns he's supplying, all pending his assurances for my safety. Lungile believes that Frankie is being prideful and I agree, which means Frankie is going to do something stupid first before something rational. But I'm hoping the offer has gone through enough ears by now to temper Frankie's pride.

After a brief argument with Lungile, he decides to go to town with me but he tells me that he can't promise that he can control his temper like last time; no surprise there. It's a risk I have to take. There can't be any changes in the parties during a negotiation, something my trainer thought me. And if it doesn't go well again and Frankie has someone in town, I will have deadly bodyguard by my side; something the streets taught me.

After I lock my door, I walk to Nia's door and knock on it. "Nia, I'm leaving for town again with Lungile, but our friends will stay in the second floor. Keep enjoying those cable channels."

"Ok, cool." She answers though the door. I understand the distance. Nia has been keeping to herself since Lungile's arrival.

Lungile joins me on the first floor. With a head nod we walk through the back exit and walk to the parking lot. As I adjust to the immediate exchange of air conditioning to the outdoor heat, two white men wearing sunglasses, blue bullet proof vests over their t-shirts, dirty blue jeans, and army boots run out from behind Miguel's truck. They point something at us that looks more like extensive water guns than normal guns.

The man with a beard yells, "Hands in the air mother fuckers!"

My heart races as Lungile and I both go for our guns, but a stream of pepper spray flows into our eyes. I would start laughing with relief because the men are either cops or bounty hunters, but the stinging pain in my eyes makes me drop to my knees. I cover my mouth to prevent any of it from going inside, but a rough pair of hands disarms me, put my hands behind my back, and put cuffs on me. They then, thankfully, pour water over my eyes.

"Your bounty is going to pay my mortgage, thanks," the bearded man says, his voice sounds happy.

Bounty hunters, perfect. "Hey guys, do me a favor. Do you see red dots on your chest right now?"

"Oh, are you talking about your friends on the second floor? The cute bellgirl let us in the back twenty minutes ago while you were taking a shower. As soon as your friend left the room, my guys should have come out of hiding and pounced on your friends."

"The bellgirl let you in, huh?" I make a mental note to get some payback on her.

"Yeah, that's right, the bellgirl sold you out. And don't worry, we'll find Ms. Smith, no matter where she's hiding."

Nia escaping is comforting news. It's just as good as the water when finally does its job on my eyes. I struggle to keep my eyes open, but when I finally able to I can see that Lungile is handcuffed as well and his face is wet with water as well. Lungile looks back at me with angry, red eyes; I think he's telling me that either I or the bounty hunters are in trouble upon his release.

As the bounty hunters continue to laugh behind us, they stand us up. And in that moment Maria, Tina's partner, walks from behind a nearby car and walks towards our direction, pointing two black Spanish Colt 44 pistols at the bounty hunters.

"What the fuck is this?" The bearded bounty hunter yells before she fires both guns and I feel the grip the bounty hunter had on my wrists slip away.

I look back and the bounty hunters are bleeding badly through their arms. She twirls the pistols on her pointer fingers before sliding the guns into her leather hip holsters. She walks to the bounty hunters, grabs their keys, and unlocks our handcuffs.

"This is our grab bitch!" The bearded bounty hunter yells.

As soon as Lungile is free, he lunges at the bounty hunters and kicks them in the chest and face until I pick him up and pull him away. "Ok, enough!"

"Let go of me! Nobody grabs me!" Lungile erupts.

I let him go just as the hotel door swings open and three more bounty hunters run towards us pointing handguns in our direction. Maria draws her guns and shoots the guns out of their hands before they take a shot. I don't know how that is even possible.

As I do the math on the chances of that happening, she points her gun towards the second floor window, and takes a shot. An unseen man from my sore eyes yells in pain and then screams, "Ok, we surrender, they're all yours! Fuck!"

Maria just smiles as she slides her guns into her holsters. She head nods to the bounty hunters, letting them take their hurt men away to the front of the hotel.

"Are you after the bounty?" I ask.

"No," she replies, looking around the area.

"Then, how…"

She sighs heavily, like I'm bothering her day. "Guy, get the hint. Tina recognized you when you first whistled at our asses.

My mistake was sharing the bounty news on your head with her. I share too much with her."

"It happens."

"Anyways, she told to me do otherwise. So, I've been keeping your ass alive since then."

"What…but…" I replay the past weeks.

"Yes, yes…the whole time. Your dumb ass should have left the city with you found out you had a bounty on you. Fifty thousand dollars had me scaring away a lot of people."

At least I was right about the bounty amount. "But my plan was…"

"What? Hide away until people forgot about you?" Her angry tone as her hands hover around her guns makes worry me. She notices this and stops as she crosses her arms.

"I did help you the one time in front of Miguel's house, remember?"

"Wow!" I'm taken aback by her sudden need to laugh. "When we walked by Miguel's house, you thought you were saving us? We were checking on you!"

"But those guys across the street…"

"I've studied Seido Juku for ten years, you sexist son of bitch!"

"Oh." I don't even know what Seido Juku is, but it sounds serious as I take into account her reaction.

"And cowboy…"

"Now you're calling me cowboy?"

"Remember when Tina happened to remember you, bad acting that you fell for. And her kindness with medical pills and supplies, more than a nurse would normally supply don't you think?"

"Well, I did pick up on that, but…"

She raises her hand at me briefly. "Just…don't! If you want to go against the wrath of the mob, that's on you. I got to make a phone call. I want to be relieved of duty."

As she reaches into her pocket, takes out a cell phone, and makes a call. I ask with a grin but in complete submission, "Can you tell me your professional name, please?"

She looks at me briefly with a smile before answering, "Dead eye." She turns her attention to the phone. "Yeah it's me. No, everyone is still alive…yes, he's still alive…I said…fine." I watch her take a calming, deep breath. "I said…yes, sweetie." She walks to me and hands me the phone. "Talk," she orders.

I take the phone and answer, "Hello."

Tina is on the line and barrages me with questions on my well being. After I confirm that I'm still in one piece and that Maria isn't pointing a gun to my head, I hand the phone back to Maria.

"Will you let me back in my house now?" Maria pleads, walking away from us. "I meant our house…I pay the mortgage don't I?"

"Wait, what's silver about you," I ask Maria. She turns around and smiles at me. Then she sticks her tongue out, showing off a silver stud in the center. "Does that count?"

She covers the phone with her hand. "Ask Tina about our sex life sometime." With a wink and a smile, she walks away, continuing her argument when she uncovers the phone.

Despite Maria's comment, I keep my mind on more pressing matters. I have to find Nia and we need to leave before the police arrive.

"Come on Lungile!" We pick up our guns and run inside, scaring people back into their rooms when we do. "I'll look for Nia, check on your guys."

"Ok," Lungile replies before he races up the stairs.

I see that Nia's door is already open and I run inside more with panic than concern, it's not until I run past the door do I think about hugging the walls for safety. I'm lucky though, her room is empty of the bounty hunters. "Nia! Nia!" I search under the bed, in the closet, and in the bathroom.

"DeAndre," Nia replies, but she sounds nervous.

"Nia, what's wrong?" I run out of the bathroom but stop in my tracks when I see her by the front door with the Ghost standing behind her. He's leaving enough space to show that he's pointing a gun to her back, but not enough space that I can take a quick shot at him. So, I tighten the grip of my gun in preparation, but I don't raise it.

He says, "Don't be stupid. I'm only here to drop off a phone from Frankie, which she has in her pocket."

"I'm going to kill you," I reply.

He smiles smugly at me. "No, you're not. How you doing Nia, still good?" the Ghost asks in a pleasant voice. When Nia nods her head in confirmation and tears, I grind my teeth and wait for her to move to the left so that I can shoot this bastard. "Ok then sweetie, walk slowly to your brother but close the door behind you as soon as you can and no one gets hurt."

Nia looks at me and I tell her calmly, "It's going to be ok Nia." It hurts to watch Nia slowly walk towards me, but I keep eye contact on her. "You're doing great Nia."

"Ok, now close the door Nia," the Ghost interjects.

As she whimpers, I quickly comment, "Hey girl, I got you. It's just you and me, ok? I got you." She nods her head with confirmation, grabs the door knob on the second try, swings the door shut behind her, and she starts crying.

I run to her, asking "Are you ok?"

She can't stop crying. I lean towards the door to catch the son of the bitch, but Nia anchors herself unto me.

"Don't leave me! Don't leave me!" She begs me.

As angry as I am at the Ghost, I'm not going to leave her. Especially like this. "Ok, it's going to be ok. Let's just move away from the door."

I carry her to the bed and it breaks my heart to see how immobile she is in my arms. A minute later, Lungile comes in the room with the men, their eyes have the same redness as I do but their faces are apparent with black and blue bruises.

"Is she ok," Lungile immediately asks as he looks her over. Nia merely buries her head in my chest in response.

"We'll talk about it later." I give him a head nod and he orders his men to start packing. As they leave, I watch as Lungile stays to keep an eye at the door

I look Nia over as her body is shaking uncontrollably. "We'll get out of here, Nia."

"What's the plan now, bruder?" Lungile asks restlessly.

"We get the fuck out of here, we give that fuck Frankie his phone call, and then we learn what we can from the conversation."

"And then," Lungile immediately asks.

I look at him in the eyes. "Then we take him down."

WHILE I'M paying off the front desk clerk for his silence, I see Lungile merely whisper something to the bellgirl that makes her tear and walk into the women's bathroom. I don't want to know, I just want to leave and I'm not alone in that sentiment. Lungile and his men are quick to pack up and speed away in their expensive rental cars.

Nia is already inside the truck and staring out the window when I get inside, slam the door closed, and start the engine. It worries me that she's not pestering me about my seatbelt or making any comments at all. I don't want to imagine the mental scars she enduring, so I buckle my seatbelt and drive her out of there as fast as I can. The plan with Lungile is to convene at a truck stop a few miles out. Since I can't see their cars anymore, it looks like we'll meet them there.

"How are you holding up Nia?" I take a quick look at her as she rubs her hands against each other.

"I want a gun," she comments with a painful tone I never heard her speak with, like she is worn out.

"You want a what? How about learning some self-defense?" I look at her again, but she turns away at the passenger window. I mentally kick myself for saying something stupid like that, considering my recent track record.

"You heard me," Nia replies with a little conviction.

"This situation…isn't what I want for you."

"What were you expecting?"

"You were supposed to be fine," I answer.

"Our parents…were supposed to be fine. That's what I was expecting. Looks like we're stuck with the versions of reality we have now."

I glance at her and it worries me as she tears and covers her mouth to muffle her whimpering. I rub her shoulder for a moment before I turn my complete attention to driving.

For the next twenty minutes its silence until we regroup with Lungile. We all stand outside together, looking like lost tourists. Lungile and I confirm with each other that there are no police sirens in the distance coming in our direction. Making the decision to call Frankie, I take the disposable cell phone out of my pocket and call the number on the flash card it came with.

"Hello, is that you…you shit?" Frankie's voice is loud and anxious, sounds about right to me.

"We were already calling each other Frankie, why the dramatics?"

"Shut up and listen," he yells. Then I hear the sound of someone mumbling and then three shots fire. The mumbling stops and my mind races with a list of names, I stare thankfully at Nia who is looking back at me with concern. "There you fuck, we're even!"

After a hard swallow, I ask, "What did you do?"

"I took your big friend, beat his ass down, and shot him in the fucking head!"

My heart beats fast as my hand tightens around the phone. "You're dead."

I hear another shot on the phone and it makes me slightly jump in place. "There, for good measure!" Frankie yells before laughing.

"I'm coming for you." There's another shot. The sound of Frankie laughing gets louder and makes me grind my teeth. "I'm coming for you Frankie!"

"Oh yeah, tough guy, you're coming for me?"

"I'm going to hunt you down and kill you!"

"Then come and get me tough guy, I'll be waiting for you!"

I throw the phone to the ground. Not happy that it didn't break into enough pieces, I take out my gun and shoot it dead center.

Chapter 14: Sending A Message

IT'S LATE BY the time we arrive at Miguel's house, sometime after ten o'clock when I take a quick glance at the clock on the radio display. There is no police tape to keep people out and no sign of the O.G.s lighting up candle vigils. There is not one car out of place that makes me nervous and I don't know why considering the circumstance.

It appears that Lungile has the same idea as I do as I watch him order his men to search around the house. They report back with the same message, no signs of strange entry points from force or bullet shells on the ground. I walk to the front door with my handgun at my side and Nia walking behind me. I sigh when I see her take out an old, black Walther P22; I bought it per her request fresh off the streets.

Reaching for the door knob, I mentally prepare myself to be the first to identify Miguel's body. Suddenly the door opens and I see a rifle in my face.

Nia jumps to my left side and points the gun towards my attacker, "Freeze!"

Her moment of bravery is taken away as she drops the gun and covers her mouth from shock. As her gun tumbles down the steps, I'm thankful that it is empty of bullets; per my foresight she would do more harm than good. Although, I'm more thankful to see Miguel standing in front of me, alive and well. As he puts his rifle down, we share a bro hug with a double back tap combo. I watch Nia remain still until Miguel hugs her carefully and then she hugs him back.

"Stick to your rosary beads, little mama," Miguel says patting her little back.

"Ok," Nia replies. She starts crying, hugging him tightly; like her faith is restoring through him.

Miguel looks around at Lungile and his men. Then he looks at me. "You got the mystery calls too?"

"What calls," I ask.

Before he can answer our attention turns to fireworks launching into the sky, making loud whistling sounds. As the night sky lights up with cascading white and red twinkling dots, my stomach turns. I trace the launch to the backyard of the white painted house across the street. It is too random a time and too late in the night to launch fireworks. The sound of motorcycles riding in the distance to our position confirms my fears.

"It's a trap!" I yell at the top of my lungs.

Gun fire comes from the windows from the house across the street. Lungile and his men duck by their cars for cover. Miguel pulls Nia and then me inside the house before going inside himself. He closes the door behind him as his house windows are shot out. I look Nia over as she clings to me. She's freaking out, looking at me for instruction. I sit her down by the door as more bullets fly pass us.

Miguel stands up, makes several shots with his rifle out the window, and sits down by the door. "The guys you brought are going into the house across the street, but the motorcycles are parking in the front of the house!"

"They must know we took cover inside the house, so they're going for the stronghold first and then they'll mop up the rest!"

"You sure, bro," Miguel asks, reloading his rifle with bullets from his shirt pocket as more gunfire is spread throughout the house.

"I'm sure! I've seen them do it a hundred times!" I look at Nia and order, "Go downstairs! Stay low to the ground!"

She does what I say, crawling to the door and running downstairs as fast as she can. It's good that Lungile and his people are taking care of guys from across the street; it gives us a chance to press the motorists into a corner; all we need to do is survive to that point.

"You ready?" Miguel asks, preparing to stand up.

I prepare to stand up myself and give him a head nod. We stand up and walk to opposite ends of the door. I prepare to shoot out the window but I see that the motorists are standing side by side in leather jackets and yellow neon stripes. They are carrying different machine guns in their hands and pointing them at the door and windows.

"Oh shit," I exclaim before grabbing Miguel and pulling him down to the floor before they spray the front door and the house with bullets, drilling more holes in the wall and furniture; although, the front door is still standing in one piece.

We quickly get up and return fire and kill three of them. I'm happy to watch them scatter as their machine guns overheat and jam, but my happiness is taken away when Nia screams in the basement as the electricity is cut off.

"Shit, it's Nia," I exclaim.

"Check on her, I got this! We got them running scared!" Miguel yells happily.

"You sure, man?"

"They shot up my fucking house man, I'm getting some payback. I got this brother."

I tap his shoulder, stay low to the floor as I make it the basement, and then quickly walk down the steps as my eyes start to adjust to the dark. "Nia," I whisper.

"DeAndre," Nia cries out as she walks into the moonlight from the corner of the room, making me briefly point the gun at her from the scare. A shotgun burst upstairs makes us both jolt in place, following that is a thump. "What the hell was that?" She yells. I just point the gun at the door, I'm afraid I know the answer. I hold my position in place with both hands on the gun as I hear several footsteps enter the house on the creaking wood above me. The voices are too low and erratic in their conversation to be Lungile and his men. "Please be ok, Miguel, please be ok, Miguel," Nia says in a low tone as if in a prayer.

One set of footsteps is walking toward the door but walks past it. Then I hear the television fall unto the floor. I keep my position as there's an argument and then I hear a feminine voice barking orders, the damn Hyena; which means that Miguel has to be dead.

"Damn," I mutter. I don't know if the O.G.s are on patrol or dead, if Maria is going to come to the rescue like before, but if Lungile survives then we have a chance.

I see flickers of light by the door before the knob twists and the door slowly opens wide. I shoot the unfamiliar face lit briefly by a flashlight in one hand as he slowly peeks inside with a hard to recognize handgun in his other hand. Nia briefly screams, making me cover her mouth as the body falls and slides down the stairs. As the gun he was carrying drops under the stairs, the flashlight bounces off the stairs and then rolls on the ground near my feet. I uncover Nia's mouth as the body stops in the center of the stairway, the head looking at us because of a broken neck.

"Yeesh," Nia says as she bends down and grabs the flashlight.

"Leave it, they'll see us!"

"I can't see shit!" She wipes the dust and blood on the flashlight unto my pants, stands behind me, and then points it forward with trembling hands.

I'm too anxious to argue right now. "Just…point it at the door." She does and the beam of light dances back and forth. "Nia…"

"What?"

"Count to ten."

"What, why?"

"You're going to give me a migraine. Count…one, two…"

"One, two, three…"

"Slower, please."

"One…two…three…four…" she counts as her hold on the flashlight gets better while I keep my position steady and my gun ready. "Can we just go now?"

I shush her and listen to the yells upstairs. I think they're cursing at me in their language, taunting me into making a mistake, like wasting my bullets in a manly barrage. That's not going to happen. My patience is punished with two flaming Molotov cocktails thrown in my direction. I push Nia back and move to the side just as the bottles smash on the floor six inches away from me, but it gets onto the furniture and wall.

"Help me!"

I turn and see that some of the back splash partially spilt on Nia's legs. Her panic adds to mine as I rush over and smother the flames on her legs with a nearby, fold up bed cover. I move the cover aside and look her legs over with the flashlight. Her gray sweats bear ugly, brown burn marks as well as her legs, but it's not too bad.

"It hurts, it hurts, it hurts," she screams and tears up.

I calmly shush her as I put the flashlight down to the floor. I move up the legs of her sweats, take off my shirt, and rip my shirt in half. I quickly bandage her legs up and make sure the knot is tight and can handle movement; with her previous screams, someone is going to track us to the basement. I take a quick, calming breath, but I can't look at her for a moment; I have to stay alert. I have enough to worry about with the fire that is spreading across the floor and tables in the corner and the smoke that is rising from the fire.

After I turn off the flashlight, I ask her, "Can you get up?" I look up at her and shake her a little. I need her to get past her shock and pay attention on me.

She looks at me with watery eyes. "I…think so."

She's a mess, but I've been in the employment with worse. She screams as the basement window is shot up from the outside. The glass breaks into tiny pieces before it falls to the floor. I get up and pull her to the back wall. Nia screams and holds me tight as they continue firing their guns, breaking the granite of the walls and rattling bullets into the mattresses, the stairs, and desk with the monitor; they're good, covering almost all possible hiding places. They stop firing and I raise Nia's shirt over her mouth when she starts coughing as the smoke rises along with the fire. She holds it in place.

I keep pointing my gun at the window and wait. I suppress the burning need to cough like the pain I endured during my training in the Russian snow with numb legs and stiff arms, waiting to take the perfect shot. *Have patience, Vulture.*

I fire immediately into the arm of another unknown poking his head through the basement window. As his body falls through and tumbles to the floor, I hear people running away, yelling at each other. I take a step closer, eyeing the window briefly, and the area is clear.

As I look over the man, making sure he's not a confused O.G. member, the man looks up at me. I see by his yellowish-brown skin and rough black hair that he's not local. I shoot him in head before Nia talks me out of it. I throw the handgun aside and take the dead man's Browning BPS Hunter 28 gauge shotgun and spare shells in his shirt pocket.

"Upgrade," I say to myself, pleased for a moment until I recall the shotgun blast earlier.

I wonder if this is son of a bitch that shot Miguel. The more I think about it, the less reason I have for pointing the shotgun toward the dead man's face and firing; he doesn't deserve an open casket funeral. I quickly reload.

"My legs…hurt…"

I turn around and see that her legs, the wounds, are bleeding through my shirt. "We've got to go, keep your mouth covered."

I make sure she stays close to me as I cover our escape to the stairs carefully, even though the heat from the sizzling flames and the urgency of Nia's free hand pressing against my bare back tell me to do otherwise. As we walk up the steps, I try to minimize the sound of each creak every step makes.

As we walk pass the body I hear Nia whisper, "Father, Son, and Holy Ghost."

"Did you just do the sign of the cross for him?" I whisper.

"Just get me out of here," she whispers back to me.

I stop at mouth of the entrance and my forearm is run through with a small hunter's knife. As I yell with pain, my ears pierce from Nia's shriek. I see a pair of fat hands go for the shotgun. I point it towards the body and give it to him, both barrels.

When the body flies to ground and fumbles around until it remain still, I have a thought in my head—who the hell decides to bring a knife instead of a gun?

"Are you ok? Should we…pull it out?"

"That's what she said…ow, don't touch it!"

"Sorry!" Nia yells as she removes her tiny fingers off the grip of the knife.

I scan the room, trying to not to focus on the numbness creeping down my hand. I see Miguel lying on the floor near the front door. He's on his back, with a bloody hole in his stomach. I wish the wood splinters that are spread around his body would cover his lifeless face.

"Oh no…Miguel," Nia cries out.

The Hyena laughs at us. I trace the laugh with my shotgun outside by the door. I pray to God, the devil, and all the powers that be that she doesn't show her face until I reload; all I need is two seconds. Instead, she tosses two hand grenades inside that bounce towards our direction.

"Get down," I yell clasping unto Nia hands, preparing to lead her away.

The explosion is loud and the force pushes me over the living room table and into the wall. The last thing I think about is losing Nia's grip in my hand as she falls back down to the basement, screaming.

Chapter 15: Changes

I WAKE UP to the beeps of construction trucks outside. I look away from the sunlight from the window on my right as my eyes adjust. It doesn't take long for me to realize that I'm in a hospital. Other than the hygienic room, I have a breathing tube placed in my nose and binding around my ears to keep it steady. There are bandages all over my body, but I start to wonder about Nia. Just then a person walks into my field of vision and to my bed.

"I need you to know that I had nothing to do with it."

I look forward and see that it's the Ghost. I can't make out his clothes past his white polo shirt, but his black eye is recent.

I clear my throat before I ask, "So, how do we…"

"I'm not here to kill you."

"Bullshit."

"So I look like type that would use a shotgun?"

As he raises his eyebrow, I'm guessing he's confirming about Miguel's fate. "And?"

"I don't mess with warlords or their people. It's my experience they take things more personally than the Mafia."

That makes sense; warlords repress their own people with smiles on their faces. I try to forget what they do to people they hate. "So, you had to find out the hard way who you were dealing with. Is that what happened to your eye…a disagreement with Frankie?"

"It's from the little guy. We're...ok now. We leave each other and our safe places alone."

"So, what, you're offering your services?"

"The police are working on links with the bullets from Miguel's house to the shooting at the gym in Harlem, where we first...met."

"I remember."

"It will be a matter of time before they match your blood at both crime scenes as well."

"I see." I rub my wrists, I imagine the handcuffs they will put on me.

"I can make the bullets and the DNA tests disappear or come out unfavorable. I can also make the gun with Nia's fingerprints disappear as well."

Despite wanting to squeeze his neck, I have to accept his help for Nia's sake; my father isn't here to help us this time and we have to survive.

"How can you make it happen?"

Ghost replies, "My brothers in the police force will take care of things for you. But that makes us square, with everything."

"It's a deal. But does that include getting additional bounty hunters off my back?"

"It's already done."

"How," I ask.

I watch him as he walks around my bed and sits to the left side, his hands twitching. "Do you really want to talk about my methods?"

"No." I have enough nightmares.

"What do you remember from the hit?"

I start remembering the grenades. Then everything is a blur. I can remember my ears ringing, the heat around my body, and black smoke filling my lungs. That to my surprise, I saw a fireman reaching under my shoulders, picking me off the small pieces of glass and wood shards spread over the floor, and carrying me out of the house. I'm not in handcuffs I realize, so I imagine Miguel's camera and tapes burnt in the fire or the Ghost's people is taking care of it.

And all of a sudden I recall screaming from Nia as Miguel's house went ablaze around us. "Nia!" I partially sit up from my bed until the wires fasten to my sides with tape stop me.

As I quickly pull the tubes and wires off me, the Ghost says, "Remember, I had nothing to do with it."

"Is she alive?"

"Yes, but…"

"What room? What room?" I yell at him, the fear in his eyes scaring possible images of horror I might see.

"She's in the next room over, room 406."

I struggle to my feet as the machines beep a flat line and the nurses run in. I push them away, ignoring their requests for me to get into bed like I'm ignoring my black-and-blue body as it asks me to do the same. I step out of my room and Lungile's men stand at attention from leaning against the nurse's desk. I turn to my left, room 405. I walk forward and into room 406.

It's a small room fit for two patients, but Nia is in the room alone and is asleep. There is a vase of flowers by her bed and I don't have to guess who it's from. I walk to her left side and look her over. The bandages conceal the small abrasions on her face and her lips have a little split but its healing. And she has just as many bandages as me but it's nothing that time can't heal. I was afraid that I'd see her body with so many burns that she'd need pig skin grafts.

I take a deep breath to calm myself after that last thought. "Nia? Nia?"

After her eyes rock back and forth for two minutes as I call her name again and again, she finally opens them but squints as her eyes adjust to the sunlight.

I turn to one of the nurses staring at me. "Put the damn shade down!" The nurse looks at me with daggers, biting her tongue I imagine, but she complies. Another turns on the pale ceiling lights. I turn back to Nia and smile. "Hey, how are you?"

Nia tries to move but she groans as I see her move against the hold from the bandages around her head, hands, and waist. She tries to talk but realizes that there's a breathing tube in her nose. I stop her from touching it.

"Hey, hey…take it easy."

Nia breathes heavily as she slowly looks at me. "It hurts," she groans in a weak voice.

I get a flashback from the fire and I shiver from a cold chill running down my spine, but I keep smiling, as much as my throbbing face will allow. "You're alright." She takes a deep breath; it's a little off for my liking. "Hey, let me get the nurse to check…"

"Miguel?"

"No sweetie…no," I reply. I can't let Miguel's death overcome me and break down in front of Nia, for her sake. She closes her eyes and whimpers. I mentally tell myself to keep my composure enough times that I believe that I can. "We were…hit hard," I reply, keeping in mind our current company.

I hold her hand but she swipes it away and looks angrily at me. "It's your fault…if we only went to the police…" She starts to cough, lightly. "You're so busy making your kind of family…that you're losing your real one. Are you happy now?"

Her cough gets heavy, to the point that her body shakes. One of the nurses runs out of the room while the other looks Nia over on her right side. Nia continues to cough, moving the bed covers off her partially bandaged body. The sheet completely slides off and then we both see that her left leg has been amputated. She gasps loudly, freaks out, and yells.

"Nurse…doctor…somebody!" I can't even form a complete sentence or thought in my panic; the shock is too much.

The other nurse returns with a doctor, immediately trying to keep Nia calm, but she's too busy slapping me in the face.

"I hate you! I hate you!"

Before I can reply she slaps me in the face again. I'm speechless; this isn't one of her childish fits. I sense her hate as I see the trust in her eyes go away. She cries at first, but then starts to cough heavily. I get up, turn around, and walk out of her room and towards mine, ignoring the looks of the staff and Lungile's men. A nurse grabs my arm to support me.

"I got it!" I yell as my eyes water.

She lets go of my arm as I walk to my room. The nurse follows until I close the door behind me. I'm not surprised that the Ghost left my room; I know why. My throat tightens as I cry and let the tears fall down my face. I cover my mouth to muffle the sound.

Nia is meant to bare the good things in life. I'm meant to be given the heartache and pain. That is our arrangement with life. She's hurt because of the life I've chosen. Something has to change, anything, for her sake. She's the only family I have left and I have to protect my family.

"I SAW THE news. I told you...run away...now look where you are. And that poor girl...is all messed up because of you. That's on you, DeAndre."

The Ghost and Lungile look at me as I pull the phone away from my ear and whisper curses about Tony, gripping the hospital phone so tightly in both hands that I'm afraid I'm going to break it. I'm already at my wit's end from getting his number from Tanya, a short but awkward conversation.

I place the phone back to my ear. "With respect..."

"Shut up, tough guy! What's stopping me from sending every guy I've got to finish you off?"

"Other than keeping my silence from the cops asking me questions and the hospital staff watching me? I have my people from Africa here and the Ghost you sent after me." I'm not sure if the Ghost shakes his head at me for outing him or for verbal peacocking, but Lungile grins—approval for me to keep going. "Or how about the fact that those items for the Queen's job you gave your friends were shit and we both know it."

If the cheap, second rate guns the bikers were using had better aim, didn't jam, or overheat I would be six feet under. If Nia's situation was better, she'd be sitting in with us for this conversation, stating that the rosary beads she hanged above the door made the guns jam.

"Where do you get the balls?" Tony yells at me.

"I have nothing but respect for you, Tony. That's why I told the Africans that you'll be a good guy to re-establish the deal with, directly."

Tony's pause confirms that I have his attention. General Abasi can buy guns anywhere. Who he trusts his time and money with isn't that simple, as I'm sure Frankie is learning real fast. If Tony bites on my offer and renews the deal, he knows he'll look good for taking care of business that Frankie messed up.

"Directly to me you said?"

"So, Tony, I take it…"

"Ok, smart guy, what do you want?"

"We keep the deal plus ten percent, and my friends from Queens get a sample of the next shipment for the friends they lost." O.G.s shot in the alley is something that doesn't get forgotten by the LCF.

"Oh, really? That wasn't even us technically."

"It was your orders. But hey, think of it as tapping into a new market. If everyone plays ball, there's no issue of payback and everyone lives to be a living example of not to mess with the Mafia."

"Yeah…well, I was thinking thirty percent, our way."

I understand. Respect and permission gets thornier the higher one goes up the ladder. "That can happen, but then we want permission to handle the problem our way."

Tony laughs. "Whatever you taking, double it…holy shit…" He keeps laughing.

"They are ready to work with you on my word and you can tell the powers that be that their budget issues are taken care of." I forgot what the code was for Mafia bosses, but I think I get the message through after he stops laughing.

"For me to even ask…"

"Tell them that if this gets done, they're good with my friends from Queens. No kickbacks, but if you want to sell to them you can, no problems. Just make sure your friends in the police get me and my people off their radar for awhile. We do all the work. I just need you for vouch for me."

With the police watching Queens now, the O.G.s gave me the ok to get payback on their behalf; I'm taking orders from them, just like the good old days. But nothing gets down until the approval is given and I need a representative on my behalf.

"You understand, they might just say no. You know that, right?"

"That's why it's good to make friends." I know they'll say no. I also foresee that they'll ask Frankie to lay low for a while, and that's where I'm banking that his reaction will make their decision more favorable for me.

I smile as Tony takes another dramatic pause. I imagine he's thinking where his loyalty lies. That he could send someone to kill me, but not being able to offload black market rifles for millions worth of blood diamonds will look bad, especially in this economy and political pressure over domestic gun sales. Pride and ego is expensive to have in the gun trade.

"Give me a second, DeAndre."

I'm taking a risk with Tony, but I've seen him put the crew's interest before his own time and time again, so his word has weight. I look at Lungile and Ghost, giving them a wink and smile. The Ghost looks uneasy in his seat, but he assured me earlier that the prospect of getting paid large amounts money is calming much of his fears.

"If I get you permission to do this thing—if—what are you going to do?"

"Take care of family business."

Chapter 16: The Big Hit

IT IS NO surprise to anyone that Frankie couldn't stay away from Manhattan. He's been running some sort of scam from a social club on Grand Street in Little Italy. Tony didn't go into the details of the scam, only that Frankie did it without permission.

I imagine it had something to do with screwing with the law-abiding Italians, African-Americans, and Chinese working in the area to make an honest buck, perfect marks. The details don't matter to me. All it means is that the scam wasn't smooth enough to keep below radar and after it was confirmed, no one up the chain was getting a taste of the money Frankie was making or was getting bribed to keep quiet. I got the go ahead to kill him; even loyalty has its credit limits.

In the meantime I have been healing for the past two weeks. I've also put on a few pounds eating takeout food, not back to my fighting weight, but I'm able to do what I came here to do. Plus the prescribed painkillers and lotions that Tina provided, I'm getting help with my pain, bruises, and burn marks.

It didn't take much to get a network of lookouts to get his routine down as Frankie passes through back and forth from his million-dollar condo on Broome Street like clockwork. But, when the night for the operation finally comes, it rains. As I watch water cascades in the wind and against the window screen in all directions, I want to laugh. Already set up in a two-floor apartment I rented, I sit in the dark. Black Widow is in my hands and still smells like the hot chocolate packets it got smuggled with; God help me, it's making me hungry.

I still have a great view into Frankie's loft through my living room window. There is no need for my walls to be cascading with charts, graphs, and pictures for an alternative plan. There were two ways we were going to do this. Plan A is the Hail Mary pass; I identify Frankie in an isolated room with no witnesses and I take him out. Plan B is the bull rush charge; we go in, isolate him, and eliminate him.

So far, Plan A is shit. It's not only raining but he's also having a party. People are listening to music and pleasant conversation. I've been listening to beads of water that have been beating against my window screen for hours. It has been difficult trying to identify Frankie, even with my night vision scope. Even when I do, I assume he's either going to be with his young woman of the night or socializing around too many people. My thoughts turn to Nia. I imagine her saying something like it's a sign from God.

I identify all important entry and exit points before I order, "Plan B, everyone."

Things are going to be different now, messier, but I'm still in charge. Plan B involves everyone having an earpiece with two-way communication, a bulletproof vest under their shirts, and silencers on their guns. They've brought their own masks, painted with white skulls, red demon horns, or whatever they creature image to their liking. In return, no innocent targets are going to be hurt. I hear Nia's voice in my head for a moment, saying that they're people and not targets.

"Alright, blue team, do your thing."

More men from Africa flew into New York over the past few days, so I love that I'm watching a sizable group of veteran soldiers run out of their parked SUVs, shoot, and kill Frankie's outside guards with a skillful, murderous simplicity.

I see more lights get turned on inside the condo at different times.

"Kill the lights," I order.

The group cuts the power and the landlines, but I see cell phones being used by fearful women looking out the window. I wish that I'm able to shoot the phones out of their hands, but I'm not going to take the risk because this weather is shit. Instead, I shoot the vases near them; that's close enough to make them scream and run away, dropping their phones in the process.

My earpiece picks up more high-pitched screams; blue team is inside. Considering the rural area, the cops won't be far behind after receiving a hailstorm of calls, so they have to find Frankie before things get complex. I watch them do their jobs as I catch a few of them running past the windows, scaring people into running out the back. I'm thankful to see that no guest wants to play hero. They are either staying down and out of the way or running for their lives.

Not that I expected them to play hero. From the looks of the white button-down shirts, ironed cotton pants, and business skirt suits, the guests look like they work in the Financial District; I guess Frankie's scam is bigger than I thought.

After I see that process repeat itself for a few minutes, I finally watch Frankie's crew run outside and I pick them off one by one, but I'm only getting their legs and arms.

"Come on." I adjust my aim for wind and go back to doing one-shot kills. "There we go."

They weren't perfect shots through the head; some went through the neck and chest, but it makes blood blurt out in different directions, confirming vital spots have been ruptured; the rain washing the blood away makes the scene look less horrifying than it really is.

Frankie doesn't show up, but two of his men run toward my apartment as someone provides cover fire from behind a parked car. I can't tell who they are because of the damn rain. Uncertainty is a bitch and she's fat and ugly.

"Shit, they're running fast."

The shooter continues to takes shots at me but only hits the outside of the window frame. After the shots stop, I quickly scan the parked cars and see a man in a suit hiding behind a car reloading his gun. I aim at his large chest and take a shot. The bullet flies through the windshield and into his chest. As he falls to the ground, I confirm that it's just a hired gun; for a moment, I thought Tony had doubled crossed me.

There's a bang from gunfire at the front door below me. "Ghost, Lungile, we have company," I whisper.

The Ghost and Lungile, red team and my silent back up, get out of the chairs behind me and run out of the room. I jump slightly as the door bangs and look back as the door shakes against the wall until it stops. I go back to scanning the house windows. Frankie has to be hiding now; he's too smart to be a lemming.

I continue to scan the windows. "Come on…where are you?"

Whispering into my ear, the Hyena says, "I'm right here."

She takes a hold of by my back and waist, picks me up, and throws me up into the air as the chair I was sitting in topples onto its side on the floor along with Black Widow. As my body is boomeranged back down, I see that I'm falling into the Hyena's, wet arms as she helps gravity drill my body to the floor. My face partially skids against the carpet, but the burning sensation on my face doesn't measure up to the aching pain from my back.

In my daze, my mind keeps replays Nia yelling at me that she hates me. The Hyena laughs as she sits on top of my chest and punches me in the face. After a few punches, I'm left prone.

"Is that all you got, big man?" The ringing in my ears doesn't prevent me from hearing how exotic her accent is and how demeaning her tone is. "The big, bad hitman."

I laugh at her, even as I taste my own blood. "I can't wait for you to die."

"You're going to kill me, big man?"

"Can you give me a minute?"

She breathes heavily over me in a fashion befitting an animal and makes my squirm as she whispers, "Scream for me." I watch in dread as she prepares to punch a hole through my head, but she pauses as the lights are turned on and she turns to her left. She asks simply, "The child?"

I sigh with relief, but imagine Lungile walking into the room with his machete in hand, covered in blood, and very upset that she just called him a child. "That's Lungile," I comment.

Upon his return with a scar on his face, an unanswered question hit me. But the answer came to full realization when I once asked myself who brings a knife to a gunfight. The answer is simple: when you plan on doing terrible things to someone. I imagined that Lungile did his duty for the general against the Hyena, hired by the rebels. And she didn't like that one bit, but Lungile escaped with a lucky shot somehow; I make a mental note to get that story from him when he's in a good mood. But now their paths have crossed again for the big pay back.

To my surprise, she stands up and laughs as she charges at him. She could have killed me, but then again I'm not exactly going anywhere. I can't even see the fight, because it hurts to move right now. But I hear the fight between the two titans to my right. I hear the grunting sounds of faces and stomachs getting hit, screams from the snapping of bones, furniture being rearranged from tackles and flips, heavy breathing from holds, and the gargling sounds of a throat getting cut by metal.

Then I hear a thump of a body hitting the floor. There is a silence for a moment, but then all I could hear is Lungile grunting as he swings his machete into the Hyena's body over and over again. I'm annoyed, as I'm still lying on the floor, but I understand. They left their impressions on each other and he has his chance to finish her off, to make sure she dies his way.

But still, I'm lying on the floor with a broken, beaten body. My parents are dead, my best friend is dead, and my sister is in the hospital; my pillars of support have been reset too quickly and too many times. And I'm numb as Lungile is hacking up the Hyena's body, copying her fiendish laugh; I change my mind, I don't want to know what he went through with her.

My thoughts turn to Nia again. If she had her way, she'd say something cliché to me right now about hitting rock bottom and it'd be the truth. I'm tired of all the death that comes with being a hitman and the guilt that follows; I can't pretend it isn't there anymore. After this, I'm done with this life; it stopped being fun a long time ago. I finally accept it; I owe an apology to my father.

Ghost walks towards me with a horrid expression, confirming to me his reason why he fears the militia. I should be laughing about Lungile leaving me by myself or joking about how he picked his need for revenge over me, but I'm not myself right now. As the Ghost helps me up, I avoid looking at Lungile's handy work. I hear through my earpiece that the blue team has found Frankie's bodyguard. I hear him arguing and yelling curses at them, calling them names that shouldn't be said when people have guns to your head.

"Get him to talk."

I pick up Black Widow and the chair, sit into position at the window, and look through my scope.

The man is disarmed but when he struggles for his freedom and punches one of them I knew he was dead.

"Don't…"

They are way past the point of no return as I watch the blue team take several steps away from the bodyguard and fill him with holes. It is a perfect firing squad execution, something that they are all used to doing since the age of twelve. They stop firing when he slowly turns around, slides off the glass on his own blood, and falls to the floor. I wanted to save him. God damn it, I want to save somebody.

In my moment of identity crisis, suddenly an SUV crashes through the garage. "Shit!" I shoot at the tinted windows and it bounces off. "Armored…everyone, evacuate…target is moving to a new location!"

I stand up, grab Black Widow, jump over the beheaded trophy Lungile has made, and run out; I make a mental note to have the soldiers clean up Lungile's mess later. Lungile and the Ghost follow me. We've got to chase Frankie down. We can't let him slip through our fingers, because if I know Frankie he's going to one place and one place only.

AFTER I GIVE Tony a call, I know he'll be ready for Frankie. I also know that if Frankie gets away and kills anyone important, I'm done for. We break more road rules than I have fingers getting to the Bronx and, when we finally got to the Lucky Guy, there is already a shoot out in progress. I scan the litter of dead humanity on the ground. No one of significance from what I can tell, well, to Mafia, at least. Their family would say otherwise; Nia's influence is in my head again, her past wisdom is giving me a slight headache.

As soon as we turn onto the street, we get shot at from two of Frankie's guys hiding in their armored SUV covered in bullet smudges. They are shooting wildly; they are dead men walking and they know it. Why drag it out further? The soldiers grant them their wish by launching a rocket from a surface-to-surface anti-vehicle missile launcher, guerilla tactics 101 and a surprise gift from Abasi.

The impact is immediate and the explosion partially makes the SUV lift into the air for a moment before it slams back down as a metal fireball. If God is good, they died upon impact. The rain controls the heat from the fire as the soldiers yell with joy at the spectacle, but they stop as they hear a woman's voice yelling. Not just any woman—it's Tanya.

I turn to the club and see Frankie walk out the front door with Tanya as a hostage. Both their faces are tattered and beaten, but Tanya is also crying. Frankie shoots inside, yelling, "Take that you back-stabbing, fat…stand still!" He keeps Tanya steady by the waist as she stops struggling.

I stay inside the vehicle but position Black Widow as Frankie uses Tanya as a human shield. "Come on, show me your head." I'm to his right; if he moves to the left or keeps moving forward I can take him out.

"Mandela! Are you out here? I got your favorite girl!" Frankie scans through the soldiers pointing their weapons at him.

He takes a step closer as the soldiers move in. "No one make a move! I got this!" They listen and back away from Frankie.

Frankie grins. "Yeah, you're out here, Mandela. You're out here, Mandela!" He moves his free hand around her neck. She gasps. "Show your face, punk!"

I adjust my aim, keeping in mind the rain and the wind. "Come on."

"I'm going to kill her, then I'm going to kill you, and then I'm going put your sister out of her misery!"

I put two shots into his skull, for good measure; I hate bullies. Tanya screams as Frankie falls dead to the ground; every king dies.

Tanya continues to stand there, crossing her arms over her stomach as Lungile confirms the kill. She looks around for me, like Urola whimpering when she knows she did something wrong. I watch as the rain makes her dress stick to the curves of her body, loosen the v-neck cut, outlines her chest, and falls down her long legs.

I want her. I want to walk to her, move the wet, black hair away from her face, and take her quivering body in my arms like a romance movie with a Nancy Wilson or Sheryl Crow song playing in the background. I want to kiss her until her toes curl. I want to take her to bed and make her mine. End credits.

In reality, I would be Tanya's man for an hour and then she'd move on. It's what she does, it's just business, and I've got to walk away from that life as well. I watch as Tony walks out of the club with a handgun in hand; only his clothes have undergone any damage. He embraces her and she hugs him back. That's where she belongs. I catch his eye and wave at him. He does the same.

"Continue with the plan gentlemen," I order through the microphone.

"You got it bruder," Lungile replies happily.

With Frankie and his men dead, Lungile and his men knows what to do. They quickly replace their guns with Lungile's weapons. The police needs bodies and a way to close their case for the recent shootings; we're going to give it to them. The newspapers will summarize the crimes as a local drug deal leading into bloodshed. The Mafia's major gun distribution isn't hurt, just Frankie's records and stash at his house; whatever will be allowable by Mafia anyway. The Ghost's people will tie everything else up in a nice package to their superiors.

I sigh when I see the soldiers start picking pockets from the dead bodies; I'm not going under arrest over pocket money. "Everyone, leave that shit alone! Let's go!"

The only really listen when Lungile yells and hits them; I see who really is in charge. With everything in place, we leave Tony to the cops and his destiny.

Chapter 17: The Ends Justify The Means

I'M HAPPY that I'm in the same hospital for physical therapy, one floor under Nia. That and being able to use their disposable razors to shave the fuzz off my face on a daily basis, like a normal human being. Through my exercise, I think about the police that was still looking for leads on Frankie's hit three days ago until the SUV explosion was explained away as a mechanical error with the engine and gas line.

Not the greatest of covers, but it works for me; if there was an undercover officer in Frankie's, he or she would have made their presence known by now. I mostly wonder if Tony is going to send someone over to kill me to cover their loose ends, but that would have taken less than three days to do.

After the trainer is done with my torture, a cool breeze finally blows out the window, a nice comfort since the air conditioning broke when I started this morning. As my trainer leaves the room, Tony walks in with Tanya clung to his arm. Their uptown attire makes me look over my sweaty shirt and boxer shorts. I stop caring about my appearance when the collective smells from their cologne and perfume invades my nostrils.

Tanya is still a vision, but I limit my view of her after she smiles at me. I stand up straight, even though it hurts to move. It hurts to breathe since the prescription pills didn't get renewed, but I don't blame Tina. I've already made a mental note to write to Congress about health reform.

I shake hands with Tony as he walks to me; Frankie's pinky ring lightly scrapes my hand, Tony's defective trophy. "Hail to the new king."

"Cut that shit out," Tony says. I can tell he likes the idea of being captain by the proud look in his eyes and grin.

I take a look out the door as it closes. I see, through the door window, two thugs is suits standing in front of the door like security guards.

"How is your sister, she alright?"

I look back at him. "She's doing better."

"Yeah, yeah, I understand. So, well…your friends from the South ready to play ball now?"

"Yeah, but I'm going to phase myself out and will bring in the Ghost."

"The Ghost? Oh, you mean John…um…John Wesley."

I make a new mental note to make fun of the Ghost later. "Yeah, well, he can handle himself, but he's young so he'll work cheaper. It'll look better if a different guy is running the trade after the thing anyway."

"You sure? Maybe you got hit too hard in the head or something?"

He's too amused at himself; getting an ego didn't take long. But I still smile. "I'm going to do more independent security. There's always someone with money that needs protection from scary people like me. No worries, I'll keep myself busy." I think that's enough confirmation for him to show that I won't be trouble in the future.

"Good man. But help me out here and explain to me why the hell your friends in the South are so loyal to you? I just want to make sure we have an understanding."

There's some of the old Tony left after all. "Have you ever heard of the term 'Ubuntu'?"

"No."

"Just think about how cool we are and do the same with them, only better."

"Sure, sure," Tony says, laughing. We hug quickly; the end of my contract with the Mafia has been confirmed. "You keeping busy in the meantime, or what," he asks as I walk him and Tanya to the door.

"I'm going to take care of my family. A friend of mine from Queens had a girl that's going to have his baby in nine months. She was going to give it up for adoption, but I convinced her otherwise." I don't mind telling him stuff that he's going to research later anyway; information is one thing the Mafia values.

"Yeah, well...I hope you get your act together." I see the concern in his eyes for his new prize.

"That's where my sister comes in." I look straight at him and smile, thankful for his calm smile.

"That's beautiful. God bless, then."

Tony waves goodbye as he opens the door for Tanya. After she walks away, I add, "By the way, if you need a carwash in Queens, my friends will give you a good price."

"Christ...yeah, sure," he says before laughing and walking out with his goons following behind him.

Talking about the baby arrangement out loud makes me realize that I didn't tell Nia. I take a moment, enough time to make sure that Tony and Tanya have left the floor. Then I take a trip to Nia's room, my first attempt to see Nia since her arrival. I open the door, wishing I had flowers and chocolates to give her. But I have nothing, just a whole sad sack of me.

I open the door and see that she's praying with the hospital priest. "I'm sorry, I'll just…"

"No, DeAndre, stay," Nia says humbly.

I watch as the priest blesses her and then gives her a hug. He gets up and walks away, giving me a pat on the arm before he walks out the room, closing the door behind him. We smile at each other, but after I glance at her amputation I briefly look away. Too often I see things that remind me that there are truly evil people in the world, and then I see Nia about to put her life together after a tragic event. It reminds me of what our father once said about the difference between God and the devil during times of strife, character.

"Hey you," I say to her, mentally hating myself for being momentarily dense.

She smiles at me. "Hey. Is it over? I mean…everything," she asks.

"Everything is taken care of."

"Do we have to lie low from the police now?"

"The police won't come after us. No one comes after us, ok?" The only issues I think she will have are social. People talk and they'll know how she lost her leg and will be polite to her in public, at best. But she's tough, I believe she will see through any bullshit and call people out on it; she does it so well with me.

"Yeah, I get it."

"Listen, I…"

"I'm sorry, DeAndre."

"Wait…what?"

"I apologize for yelling at you and saying that that I hate you."

"You forgive…me?" My eyes are swelling with tears as she signals me to her and I obey. We hug a good, long hug. "I'm sorry…I'm sorry…"

She kisses my head three times and then hugs me tighter. "It's ok. I still love you."

"It's all good, Nia. I took care of everything…you, me, and Miguel's baby."

"What…what do you mean by that?"

"I set you up to adopt Miguel's baby in nine months," I say quickly.

"What…what!"

Her tiny arms tighten around my neck, surprisingly harsh, and I gasp for air. "Ah…Nia…you're choking me…" I give her the universal signal for release by tapping her arm, but she doesn't release her hold.

"You did what?"

I reach for the communicator switch and barely hit the button as I gasp out, "Nurse…nurse!"

Nia lets me go as the nurse, someone new in the rotation and unfamiliar to our shenanigans, enters the room. I fall onto a nearby chair as I gasp for air. "Nurse, I want this woman arrested for assault and battery!"

She simply shakes her head with disapproval as she walks away and closes the door behind her.

"Of all the stupid, pig-headed, narrow minded…"

"Really?"

"…inconsiderate, sexist…"

"If I had a dollar…"

"…dim witted…"

"There's more?"

"…pig-headed…"

"Read the dictionary much?" I see her eyes water and I back off the nonsense. "I thought, maybe…"

"How am I supposed to take care of a baby?" She sniffles as she looks down at her leg; just one more thing in her life that didn't go to plan.

I stand up, take a few tissues from her tissue box, sit by her side, and hand them to her. "You'll live in our parents' house and anything you need I'll help you with." I thankfully have nine months to prepare, as does she.

"But a baby…" She puts the tissues by her nose.

I put my arm around her shoulders. "If it's a boy, name him Miguel. So when he messes up, you can say stuff like…just like your father. And if it's a girl…if a girl, well…"

"I like Sophia," she says with a light smile.

"Let me see…Sophia Johnson! I told you to not mess with that boy! If you think because your birth mother is a slut that makes you a slut, I'm going to slap the truth into your behind!"

She slaps my side. "Stop it! Sophia is going to be saint."

"That's not what I heard," I jokingly whisper, looking away.

That's why I'm caught by surprise when she pushes me off the bed with a hard push. After I fall to the floor, I hear her muffled laugh. I look up as she uncovers her mouth and says, with a smile, "Sorry."

"Damn, you're strong!"

"Arm therapy for my wheel chair," she says, wiping her tears away.

"Now she tells me."

"Yeah, yeah…if I decide to do this, is Uncle DeAndre really going to present in Miguel's or Sophia's life other than the major holidays?"

"Um…"

"Well?"

"Which answer gets me less beaten up?"

"The truth shall set you free."

"The truth is going to get me into a hospital bed."

Chapter 18: The Three Doves

To FINALLY see that I have my apartment back to the quality of cleanliness I once had it before the ordeal with Frankie brings me peace of mind. Although it still pisses me off how much stuff Tony's guys stole. But its water under the bridge and a hit to my pocket, because I don't think Mafia related crimes is in my insurance plan.

As I put aside the box of pictures I picked up from Nia's house, my inheritance, there's a knock on the door and I look at my watch, one o'clock. Randel, my tattoo artist, is on time as usual. I open the door and he's standing in his usual white, short-sleeve shirt, black tie, black pants, and leather shoes. His black hair is cut short and he's clean shaved, but his pale, white skin makes me think he needs another trip to Africa.

I would make a joke that with his motorized tattoo needle and homemade ink in his silver brief case that he should be passing out religious pamphlets, but I've been making less jokes lately; that and Randel has a wrestler's body.

"Hey Randel."

"DeAndre, I'm here for your appointment." We shake hands like gentlemen before I let him in. He looks around my place. "The hit on you was taken care of, correct?"

"Correct."

"Am I in any danger?"

I like Randel, because he's very to the point and he reminds me of Miguel, but with half the sense of humor. "No, it's taken care of. How are you Randel?"

"Super."

"Ok." I laugh briefly before closing and locking the door.

"I understand. How many feathers do you want today?"

"None, you're giving me three doves above the vulture." I don't regret any of the kills I've recently made.

"Doves, that's interesting. That's the theme you're looking for?" he asks, turning to me.

"They'll give me a sense of peace. And these will be last ones, man." I've been inspired from visiting my parents' and Miguel's graves. "I'm getting out and staying out." That is thanks to Nia's constant inspiration.

"Of course, so where do you want them?"

I turn around and point to my back. "Two on my shoulder blades and the last can go above the vulture."

"What designs did you have in mind?"

"You could make them same…I guess." I trust he can make doves look good.

"Who are the doves for?"

"Well, it's for my parents and my friend who died." I can trust him with that much information.

His cold, stern fingers trace against my back. "I can put a dove for your father with an olive branch on your left side, a dove for your mother here with a red rose on your right side, and a dove for your friend over a cloud in the center. It'll be very Zen."

"Damn, man, that sounds good." I was right, he's the man.

"Considering your situation, I'll keep it the same price, alright?"

"That's cool, man, thanks."

Chapter 19: The Story Goes On

"THE ULTRASOUND says it's a girl!"

"What? Hold on!" I pull to the side of I-95 and put the cell phone off speaker. "What did you say?"

"And Tina says hi."

I shake my head. "Yeah, hi…what was that about the baby, Nia?"

"Oh, sorry, it's a girl." Nia laughs lightly.

I smile, thinking about how poorly the kid is going to be made fun of until she starts playing basketball. "That's…awesome."

"Oh my god, you should be seeing this…she has such a strong heartbeat."

I take a minute to calm down before I get emotional. This interview is the last of my favors I have left and it was a stretch; Tanya's dog sitter knew of a client in Greenwich looking for a new security guard.

Nia continues after she sniffles, "She's so beautiful."

"I got to go, ok, but send me pictures later, ok?"

"Ok. I love you."

"Yeah, see ya." I hang up the phone and sniffle as the thought of Miguel makes my eyes water.

Picking Nia as the adoptive mother is the right choice; in my heart, I know that Miguel would agree. She always has the right mindset. Not being able to have children and getting divorced by a piece of shit husband we all swore never to talk about, never made her bitter. She instead became a teacher and found other means to give to the world by helping people. Her faith keeps her centered. She's my rock. She's my idol.

COMING from New York to Connecticut on this surprisingly warm autumn day, I see large concrete buildings at odds with brightly colored trees with red and orange leaves. To drive on roads with a blanket of mud brown leaves on them is picturesque. That I would see couples taking leisurely walks together, instead of jogging individually, is kind of sweet. But all of that is predictable, what I didn't expect to see is so many wood and stone fences by people's homes. Stone driveways and custom made mailboxes in same shape of the houses they are in front of. Marble statues of animals on olive green lawns, not that the statues are essential considering the number of wildlife I saw eating from personal gardens. And when I pass by two lush golf courses twenty minutes from each other, I just smirk.

The Voltaire mansion is something from a magazine. There are several buildings I don't know their use for, a tennis court and garden around the back, and a sitting area by a nearby stream at the side. It's fantastic.

I park in the back, as instructed to me prior to arriving, and I'm lead into the mansion by the maid. I see that Kate Voltaire, the potential client, has a life-sized collage painted on the wall. In it, she's lying on her side on soft white feathery sheets, sprinkled with fresh rose petals.

The matching red bra and panty set she's modeling fits perfectly on her white, airbrushed body. Her light brown hair is combed and draped to the side of her shoulders by professionals. Her legs are bent the right way, showing her toes playfully pressing against each other. In this moment, I think of the twenty pictures of my niece's ultrasound that Nia sent to keep me focused.

I have to keep my focus, her sister, Lauren Voltaire, is sitting at the kitchen table with a copy of my resume in front of her. She smiles at me as she quickly looks me over; at least I'm making a good first impression with my suit, but that's the easy part.

I look her over myself. I wonder how Lauren has the time to make her black hair drape so smoothly against her white cotton shirt. And I hate how distracting her curves are in her black pair of straight jeans. It's comforting to see that she is wearing her pink house slippers, but if it puts her in a hiring mood I'm not complaining.

After we shake hands, I sit down and endure twenty minutes of tough interview questions. But just when I start to wonder if my cover stories about my past weren't good enough, Lauren says, "You're hired."

"I am?" I bite my tongue for blurting that out.

"You're surprised?" She grins.

"Well, to be honest, Ms. Voltaire…"

"Call me Lauren," she says with a smile, showing off her pearly teeth. Just another distraction as I sit across kitchen table from her.

"Well, Lauren, I thought…"

"You drove from New York to Connecticut for an opportunity, you have a sense of humor, you're honest, and my dog sitter never had a problem with you or your checks. What's the problem?"

I know why there isn't a line of people outside; she's too intimidating even while smiling. "I want the job."

She extends her hand, I shake it, and the contract has been made. "Congratulations."

"Thank you." I hear a dog barking and a woman screaming. Lauren just sighs. "Is everything ok?"

"That's Kate and Houdini on the tennis court. You should make an introduction before you miss all the drama."

"Really?"

"Yeah, you'll enjoy it."

As I stand up, I ask, "Who is Houdini?"

She answers with a grin, "My little angel."

IT TAKES me five minutes, but I walk onto the tennis court. Kate is wearing a white shirt, tennis shorts, and black sneakers. She's also playing tug-of-war with the largest dog I've ever seen, and he's gnawing his teeth happily against the head of her racket. Kate is grabbing the handle for dear life, attempting to pull it out of Houdini's slobbering mouth with forceful pulls.

Her model frame doesn't compare to the strength of what I can see now is a full grown, gray Irish wolfhound; my experiences and conversations with Tanya's sitter has left me some useful knowledge.

"Hi, Ma'am, I'm…"

"Could you...help me out here, please?"

"How shall I..."

"Could you pin him down or throw holy water on him?"

I smile. "Your sister said that he's an angel."

"Some angel, he's going to give me a heart attack or make me pick another sport to play."

I slowly sneak behind Houdini, but his eyes spot my attempt. He lets go of the racket, runs to me playfully, tackles me down easily, and licks my face; Miguel would call this funny as hell.

"By the way, Ms. Voltaire, I'm your new bodyguard."

"Good, I need someone to keep this monster busy." I watch as Kate looks at the teeth marks and slobber on her racket in disgust. "And call me Kate."

I look at her face as she looks at me with a model's smile, and I swear that I see a sparkle in her gray-blue eyes. I swear that I see my destiny.

Tom Bourguillon is a member of the FCW (Fairfield County Writers) and has written twice for NanoWrimo (National Novel Writing Month).

He loves to write short stories in the genres of Comedy, Drama, and Romance.

For updates on his next projects, podcasts, upcoming events, or to schedule him for personal appearances, please contact him via his book's fan website at:

https://www.facebook.com/FamilyBusinessNovel

www.ingramcontent.com/pod-product-compliance
Lightning Source LLC
Chambersburg PA
CBHW021044130626
46552CB00005B/2007